The Cowboy's Stolen Heart

THE COWBOY'S STOLEN HEART

THE COWBOYS OF SWEETHEART CREEK, TEXAS
BOOK 1

JEAN ORAM

The Cowboy's Stolen Heart
The Cowboys of Sweetheart Creek, Texas (Book 1)

By Jean Oram

© 2020 Jean Oram
All rights reserved
First Edition

This is a work of fiction and all characters, organizations, places, events, and incidents appearing in this novel are products of the author's active imagination or are used in a fictitious manner unless otherwise stated. Any resemblance to actual people, alive or dead, as well as any resemblance to events or locales is coincidental and, truly, a little bit cool. Unless, of course, your name is Travis. Thanks for the teasing—you gave me some good ideas. I hope you enjoy your mayoral debut!

Printed in the United States of America unless otherwise stated on the last page of this book. Published by Oram Productions Alberta, Canada.

COMPLETE LIBRARY OF CONGRESS CATALOGING-IN-PUBLICATION DATA AVAILABLE ONLINE

Oram, Jean.

The Cowboy's Stolen Heart / Jean Oram.—1st. ed.

ISBN: 978-1-989359-27-3, 978-1-989359-28-0

Ebook ISBN: 978-1-989359-25-9

First Oram Productions Edition: November 2020

Cover design by Jean Oram

When I was a kid we'd take the Friday of the Calgary Stampede parade off work on the farm and drive into the city super early to get good seats on the bleachers set up along 9th Ave—just a few blocks from my grandmother's high-rise apartment. That was back in the day when the parade floats still tossed candy to the spectators. The parade would kick off ten days of celebrations in the city.

At some point during the summer my brother and I would be shipped off to Ontario to spend time with my other grandmother while my parents focused on the harvest. (Time spent in Muskoka led to the inspiration for my Summer Sisters series.) When we got off the plane in Toronto my grandmother would always be able to find our luggage carousel quite quickly due to all of the folks wearing cowboy hats. One year it was my brother wearing the hat. One year it was me.

Not as many folks wear cowboy hats around here anymore, but farmers and ranchers still exist. You earn your belt buckle. You have your going to town, good boots. You may even have your going to town truck.

The folks who work the land tend to be a special breed. They pause. They speak their mind, and are honest about their thoughts. They say a lot in few words. And they will still stop if you're pulled over on the side of the road, because they believe in community and helping each other. (They'll pull you out of a snowy ditch, too.)

I've alway wanted to touch on these soulful folks and this new Texas series is in their honor. To those who keep us fed, no matter the weather or the conditions in which they have to work to put food on their table as well as ours.

Happy reading,
Jean Oram
Alberta, Canada 2020

ACKNOWLEDGMENTS

A giant thank you to Margaret C., Tessa S., my beta team (Margaret C., Donna W., Erika H., Lucy J., Sarah A., Connie W.M.,) as well as my fabulous and fun error team. Also, a thank you to my mastermind group for letting me talk "Texas" and keeping me sane while my production plans got revamped and revamped again and again as COVID hit, my family overran my home office, and I became a "teacher" as well as a writer, then put our house up for sale and generally tried to change as many things as possible at once. Because who needs sanity, right?

For all those who have waited patiently for the Wylder clan to take the stage. This one's for you. (And the next four or five books, too. ;))

But most of all, for Travis W. This may not be the story Moonshine and Weiner Water as requested, but I did like the name Sweet Meadow Falls and hope you don't mind me using it as a jumping off point to create the Sweet Meadows Ranch. Enjoy your debut as mayor of the 4,123 citizens of Sweetheart Creek. May this new career treat you well.

Laura Oakes rolled down the window of her vintage Volkswagen Beetle, the tension over wondering if her car would make the twenty-seven-hour drive lifting off her. The fresh Texas Hill Country morning air filled the vehicle as she slowed at the town of Sweetheart Creek's outer limits. Its welcome sign said Population 4,123. Unless a baby had been born since July, that number was off by at least one resident.

Laura inhaled and allowed her heavily loaded car to coast over the small bridge that would take her into town. While she adored the bustle of New York, there was something about her great-aunt Luanne's hometown that made life feel more real. She wasn't sure what it was, exactly, but figured it was likely a combination of the gentle hills, the towering oaks, the women and their ever-ready casseroles, and the way men still tipped their hats in greeting. Everything here was just more... personal. The little things still mattered.

There were only a few vehicles angle parked along Main Street this early on a Saturday morning. The Longhorn Diner had been repainted since her last visit, its white wood trim looking quaint and spiffy against the red brick. The homemade

Go Torpedoes! This Is Your Year! sign hanging in the window added to the small-town Texas charm Laura had missed. She'd been back only for quick visits since the blissful month she'd spent with her aunt when she was thirteen.

Even though she was to meet Luanne's friend Nina at the diner to get the key to her late aunt's home which had been willed to Laura, she continued on through town to see what else had changed. By the looks of things not much had, and she turned around five blocks later to head back to the Longhorn.

The diner was like an old friend, a place where she'd spent many hours sitting on the tall stools along the back counter, drinking milkshakes. It had been a throwback in time even then, the thick, cold drink freezing her throat on unbearably hot days. That summer she had savored the oppressive, humid Texas heat, even though it made her hair a frizzy mess and caused her bare thighs to stick to the vinyl soda fountain stools. So simple and carefree.

She looked down at her long gel fingernails wrapped around the old steering wheel, their shiny, violent color somehow emphasized in a way it hadn't been in New York. Hussy Red. That was what the Filipino nail artist had called the shade, with an amused twinkle in her eye. Laura had agreed, loving the powerful hue and the way the perfect gloss reminded her of how far she'd climbed in the world of modeling. She had earned everything she'd wanted and more.

Well, mostly. Upon announcing her retirement from modeling last month she'd found the flicker of her fame flame had begun to quickly fade. Her friends were vanishing the same way they'd appeared—instantly. She was discovering that there was nothing like stepping out of the limelight to find out who and what were real in your life.

Her newly ex boyfriend, Memphis, was another example of that. His shift in attitude toward her had been similar to that of her yoga instructor, who had once sought her out at the end of class, but now barely gave her a nod. Her so-called book club, who mostly just drank wine and complained about their pedicurists, had forgotten to tell her about the date change for the latest meet-up, and she'd shown up on the wrong day, surprised and hurt.

And Memphis. She'd really thought he was in it for the long haul. She'd believed that how quickly he'd advanced their relationship had been due to them being in their thirties and knowing they were on the right path together. But apparently their joking about marriage and kids had been just that to him—a joke.

When she'd retired, Memphis had panicked, telling everyone she was getting some work done on the hush-hush and would soon be back, better than ever. It had been humiliating. And even though he'd begun to resent the time she'd spent away on photo shoots, he'd begged her to reconsider, to bargain her way back into modeling as if she had no shame. Like she didn't understand that models over thirty—even if they'd once been in the swimsuit edition of *Sports Illustrated*—were entering the quieter years of their career, and that it was better to bow out gracefully than to have the door shut in your face. Repeatedly.

When she'd proposed that she might become a stay-at-home mom, he'd argued that his career on Wall Street was just catching fire, and he feared getting daddy tracked. It turned out he had other reasons for being squeamish about sharing more than their lovely Hudson River-view apartment.

Laura blinked and shook away the memories as she accidentally exited town the way she'd just arrived. She sucked in a breath as she caught sight of an armadillo ambling across the road ahead. The squeal of tires as she jerked the wheel to the right was followed by a screech and thump as the suitcase she'd strapped to the roof slid over the windshield and hood, hit the pavement and skittered off into the ditch, narrowly missing the animal. The engine sputtered and went quiet.

"No-o-o!" After driving for two hours straight, the car wouldn't restart unless it sat for at least twenty minutes. Hoping for a miracle, Laura turned the key, fingers crossed. The motor whined and clunked, then gave its classic I-won't-start-until-I-have-a-rest sound.

"You poor baby. You did good. I know you're not used to being out of the garage and driving so far or so fast." She'd loved having a car in New York even though it was costly and impractical. Her friends had teased her for keeping the finicky old Beetle, but she adored it and what it represented. Having bought it with her first real modeling paycheck, she considered it a symbol of freedom and independence. She relied on nobody. Not the subway or cabs or buses. It was all her. She could grab her purse and go at any time.

Laura opened her door, digging in her purse for her phone so she could take a photo of the armadillo for her social media account while she collected her suitcase. The heat coming off the pavement warmed her from her open-toed heels up to the skirt of her fitted dress.

She started walking in a wide circle to avoid the armadillo, but it nailed her with its dark eyes, giving her chills.

Laura snapped a quick photo, then tried to shoo the animal away, since it was heading into the ditch and directly toward her suitcase, which looked as though it might be spilling its contents.

"No! Go on! Git!"

It turned to look at her and she stumbled back a step. It waddled toward her, its pace increasing. Laura hurried toward the protection of her car. The armadillo screamed at her in a low cat-like yowl and Laura tore past the vehicle, unwilling to take the time to open the door and climb in.

From what she thought was a safe distance, she turned. The armadillo was still following her, picking up speed when it saw her pause, as though hoping to catch up with her.

Laura kept going until she was in town and only a few doors

from the diner, skirting a row of bicycles and lawn mowers on the sidewalk in front of the hardware store. Her heart warmed with memories of the handsome teenager who'd worked irregular hours there the summer she'd spent in Sweetheart Creek. His skin had been tanned, and his movements so fluid and confident despite an obvious growth spurt that had put him near six feet. How tall was he now? Would he be a rare find in her world and be taller than she was?

She used to find projects around her aunt's house so she'd have an excuse to go in and ask him for advice. That had been some crush. It had given her lofty ideals about what love should feel like.

An older cowboy was walking toward her, his boots clacking on the concrete, a swagger in his step as his steely gaze swept over her.

"Good morning," she said, feeling out of place.

He tipped his hat, still taking her in. "Morning."

She shifted in the sexy high heels that felt normal in New York. Nobody wore fitted purple sundresses and Jimmy Choos around here as casual wear. They wore things like the fabulous aquamarine boots in the window of Blue Tumbleweed—and only when dressing up.

As she and the man passed each other, Laura pointedly looked away, catching sight of a faded truck parked in front of the diner that was almost as old as her car. The Chevrolet had likely been a nice bright red when purchased decades ago, but was now more a rust color, its pigment sucked out from years of being subjected to the unforgiving Texas sun.

Inhaling a fresh breath, Laura yanked open the diner door and marched to her favorite red vinyl stool at the back counter, ready for a little time and perspective that only this small town seemed able to provide.

LAURA SMOOTHED her hands along the counter, which was still white with flecks of silver stuck in it. When she had been that gangly girl with braces and out-of-control curls she would sit here watching the cook, Nina, through the open window across the gangway, where waitresses hustled back and forth with orders, coffee and dirty dishes. Almost every time Laura came in she would order a milkshake, not even thinking about calories.

She gave her head a little shake. Calories no longer mattered in the way they had even a few months ago. It felt as if her entire life was changing faster than she could keep up. She was no longer in a committed relationship, and no longer had a big career. And three days ago she'd reached her limit with Memphis and his stubborn refusal to move out of her apartment. She'd called the landlord and broken her lease, put her belongings in storage or into her little car, and had hit the road, leaving Memphis to work out a new lease with the landlord.

Meaning she was not only unemployed and single, but she was homeless, too.

She clenched her trembling hands together. She had a lot of investments set aside, and her agent had a few deals in the works that would utilize the brand she'd built around her name. There would be income, and maybe even a job of sorts to keep her from feeling as though the bottom of her life was falling out.

"Can I get you anything, hon?" asked the woman behind the counter. She fished a notepad and pen from the pocket of her apron as though expecting Laura to order an intricate meal that would test her memory skills. No gluten, sauces on the side, and substitute this for that.

Laura was so tired of it all. She just wanted to order something real.

"Just a coffee, please." She eased forward on the stool as the waitress turned to take the coffeepot off its small burner. "I'm looking for Nina. Is she in?"

"Just stepped out. Said she'll be back in about a half hour. Her cat needed his insulin shot, and she forgot to give it to him before she left for work."

The waitress, studying Laura, placed a black coffee in front of her. The brew was steaming, a thin film of oil from the ground beans swirling on the surface. Hot and bitter. It wasn't at all what she wanted, even though it was as real as it came.

"You know what? Can I get a chocolate milkshake, too? Please."

The waitress grinned with warm recognition. "I thought that might be you, Laura, but I darn near didn't recognize you with that glossy highlighted hair of yours. Look at how beautiful you've become. I heard about your success. *Vogue?* Oh, your aunt was so proud of you. God rest her ever-lovin' soul."

"Thank you." Laura felt a wash of shyness, as if she was still that kid who had been shipped from the city to spend a summer here while her parents fought their way through a divorce. It was around then that independence came to be something to strive for, even though it had scared her witless trying to figure out how to stand on her own two feet.

She eyed the waitress, who sported an unnaturally yellow swoop of teased hair above her wrinkled, friendly face. Though her posture was slightly stooped and her frame rail thin, she had an air of bustling alertness about her. "Mrs. Fisher?" Laura guessed.

The woman placed a hand to her sequined Western-style blouse, looking pleased. "I can't believe you remember me. Bless your heart, sweetie." She turned to the counter and pulled a tall metal cup from a stack, asking over her shoulder, "Can I get you anything else?"

Laura perked up. "Could I also have bacon and eggs—scrambled—and toast, sourdough if you have it. I'd like shredded hash browns, and maybe some of those delicious pancakes if you still make them. Extra syrup."

"Honey child, you gotta tell me what kind of workout you do

that y'all can eat like that and look like this." The woman let out a gusty chuckle.

"I won't look like this for very long if I eat like that regularly, but I think it's time I treated myself."

"Truer words were never spoken. Us womenfolk often forget to treat ourselves, and we're hard on ourselves, too. Well, unless we've got ourselves a no-good man. In which case they become the expert at making us feel like something out of a cow's bottom, if you know what I mean."

That was pretty much what Memphis had called her car. A piece of…

Remembering where she'd left her vehicle, Laura said, "My VW Beetle died just outside of town. Do you think it'll be okay there until I'm done eating? It's mostly off the road, luckily."

"Honey, we need to get you hooked up with Clint." The waitress abandoned the half-made milkshake and moved to the kitchen window, calling, "Do you know Clint's number at the shop? And gimme a Wylder special while you're at it."

"Who's Clint?" Laura asked.

"The local mechanic."

"Oh, the car's fine. It just needs to rest for a few minutes, then it'll start again."

Mrs. Fisher gave her an odd look. "You sure, hon? That sounds like something in need of fixin'."

"Maybe some other time."

"Well, it should be okay there for a bit, but some kind heart may tow it for you. The good thing is they'll likely come in here first to ask about it."

Mrs. Fisher called through the cook's window that she didn't need Clint's number, after all.

"An armadillo chased me. Otherwise I would have stayed with the car, or left a note that I was coming back, and not to tow it."

"Oh, that would be Bill."

"Bill?" Laura repeated. The town had named that cranky beast with the croaky scream?

"There's a drink named after him at the Watering Hole. He's ornery, so it's best you left the scene. He's not one to trifle with. Too many people have fed him and he's lost his fear of humans." Her expression became more serious, and she quietly said, "If you need anything while dealing with your auntie's estate, don't you hesitate to come in here and let me know. I'll help you out the best I can, or find someone else to, you hear?"

Laura's eyes welled with tears and she nodded, not daring to speak. She usually saw her aunt only at Thanksgiving, when Luanne would come to the city for some "razzle dazzle." Even though they got together rarely, she felt the loss, her aunt having given her space and freedom, during her thirteenth summer, when she'd needed it the most. Her aunt, in many ways, had been one of her biggest cheerleaders. Even the timing of leaving her the house here in Sweetheart Creek felt strangely fortuitous— giving her space and a comforting place to think just when she needed it the most.

Mrs. Fisher's own eyes filled with sadness as she silently patted Laura's hand before scooping it up, saying, "Well, now. Those are some beautiful nails."

"You can say it," she replied with a sigh. "High maintenance."

"They're lovely. Some of the girls go over to Riverbend to get their nails done if they're too busy at the Big Hair Salon, and it costs them a pretty penny. And their nails don't turn out half as nice as yours."

"Thank you."

Mrs. Fisher was leaning in, studying Laura's eyelashes. "Have you ever had your eyes glued shut when they're putting those things on?"

"Oh." Laura reached to touch her fake lashes before catching herself. "That's the worst part." She blushed, feeling as though the woman was noting every effort she took to ensure she always upheld the appearance of fashion model. In New York you were supposed to make it all seem natural, and as though you didn't spend weeks of your life putting it all together. And for what? To attract a man who wasn't there when you needed him.

She stopped herself from following that line of thought.

"Is it all too much?" she asked, hoping the woman would be honest with her.

"Nothing's too much if we're happy." Mrs. Fisher went back to work on the milkshake.

Laura thought about that until her shake was placed in front of her and a bell rang near the window, signaling her meal was ready.

"Order up for Miss Model of the Year," the waitress said brightly, placing a large plate of food in front of her.

Laura felt heat flood her face as she reached for a fork. "Not this year." She'd won twice in her late twenties, but that ship had sailed.

"Next year then." Mrs. Fisher smiled and passed her a syrup container.

Laura gave a small shake of her head.

"No syrup? I thought you asked for double?"

"I'm not modeling any longer."

"Why not? You could win any pageant in the state with that smile of yours."

Laura gave her a grateful look. "I've retired."

Mrs. Fisher appeared dumbfounded, a bit like Memphis had when she'd told him the same news.

"Time to turn the page," Laura said, with more enthusiasm than she felt. "Start something new."

"What are you going to do?"

"I don't know." That's why she'd told her sister she was going to spend at least a few weeks here, sorting out Luanne's home as well as her own life. Being in Sweetheart Creek had helped her find her direction once. She hoped it might again.

"You should become an exercise instructor!" Mrs. Fisher said. "I bet the pool would let you teach a class again."

Laura smiled at the memory. She'd been on an exercise kick the summer she'd spent with Luanne, and she'd convinced the pool's director to allow her to teach an aquacize class three nights a week. Several local ladies had joined her in their floral swimsuits and matching bathing caps. It had been fun, but she hadn't been particularly good at it.

"We'd all come, based on the hope you could get us all looking half as good as you do," Mrs. Fisher said, with a cheery wink that made Laura feel special. "You're a go-getter. Nothing stands in your way." When she caught Laura's doubtful expression, she added with authority, "I knew you when you were a kid. These kinds of things don't change. Now eat up. We don't want anyone saying we didn't feed you while you were in town."

2

Outside the Longhorn Diner Levi Wylder reconsidered his decision to eat in town and be social. He had parked his faded '84 Chevy in front of the place, then walked down to Clint's Parts and Mechanic to pick up a new radiator hose. He'd planned to treat himself to breakfast in town, but the thought of battling Mrs. Fisher's persistent efforts at matchmaking was an exhausting one. He needed another ranch hand or three, not a girlfriend.

His stomach rumbled, and with a sigh, he gave in, pulling open the diner's glass door. As he strode to the rear, he lifted his hat as he passed various tables, nodding and offering good-mornings.

"This the year your brothers are going to get our boys state championship rings?" asked Davis Davies, DJ and owner of the local radio station.

"Hope so." Myles and Ryan coached high school football, and for the past few years they'd narrowly missed taking home the title. The town was about ready to have a breakdown over the string of losses.

Placing his cowboy hat on the counter, Levi took a stool at the coffee bar along the back, two spots down from a woman who smelled like perfume. It wasn't overwhelming, and it was a nice scent, just out of place. In fact, every inch of her groomed body was out of place. This woman was the princess his ex-girlfriend had strived to be, going so far as to hightail it out of town with his heart, not stopping until she was well embedded in Hollywood. He'd truly thought Coulter was going to return home from college with her veterinary-assistant degree and work on the family ranch with him. But nope. She'd quit college and started acting, not letting him know she wasn't coming back until she had landed her first movie role.

"Coffee," he said to Mrs. Fisher, wishing his words hadn't come out so abruptly.

The waitress put a hand on her narrow hip and gave him a scolding look. She had been deep in conversation with the stranger, no doubt delighted to have someone new to chat with.

However, the way Mrs. Fisher eyed him now made him fear it wouldn't be long before she tried to set the two of them up, even though they obviously weren't the least bit compatible.

The newcomer glanced over at his tone.

"Coffee, *please*," he said, softening his request.

Mrs. Fisher took her time sauntering to the coffeepot, while someone slid onto the stool to his left. A hint of strawberry shampoo and lip gloss. Jackie Moorhouse. The woman meant well, but had been annoyingly and persistently available since the third grade. So far she'd done a bang-up job of chasing every eligible male out of the county. Well, except for himself and three of his four brothers. And they were definitely all in her crosshairs.

Levi shifted, turning his back on Jackie and in the process facing the new arrival. She was gorgeous. She probably used all the hot water in the morning, and hogged the entire bathroom counter, filling it with products that kept her golden hair so glossy and fine. Would it feel as soft as it looked?

He shifted again, facing the open window into the kitchen. His mother often teased him that he just needed the right woman. One who would share the burdens and joys of life on the Sweet Meadows Ranch, and wouldn't get upset at his odd hours, or the days he sometimes had to spend rounding up herds, sleeping under the stars. You'd think if that was true he'd have found someone by now, living as he did in the heart of Texas.

"Jackie?" Mrs. Fisher asked, waving the coffeepot.

"No, thanks, Mrs. Fisher. I like your shirt. Is that the one that was in the window at Jenny's?"

"It is. Blue Tumbleweed's prettiest one. Jenny said she'd ordered it with me in mind." She twisted to model it for Jackie.

Levi pitched forward on his stool and reached over the edge of the counter, fishing around for the stack of white cups. Finding one, he held it out hopefully.

"Coyotes eat your prize heifer last night?" Mrs. Fisher asked with a smirk, filling his cup before lifting the empty plate from in front of the woman to his right. It had been scraped clean. A milkshake glass in front of her had the end of its straw stained cherry red from her lipstick, which matched her long nails. Levi dared another appraisal of her, having missed the signs of a healthy appetite the first time. Was the look of sorrow in her pretty hazel eyes causing her to eat diner food in an attempt to bury sadness?

He shook off an eerie feeling of familiarity. He was pretty certain he'd remember this woman if they'd met before.

"Nope," he said, returning his attention to Mrs. Fisher. "No coyotes. Just typical ranch problems."

Ever since his mother and father had split up, then decided to retire, while sending Levi's cousin Nick Wylder off the ranch at the same time, Levi had been struggling to keep all the loose ends tied into a big knot so things didn't unravel. If they did, he'd risk sending the older generations of Wylders into poverty during their golden years, as they depended on the ranch's income, too.

His father had optimistically believed that his leaving would allow the boys to claim their birthright, but so far it had mostly been Levi, his brother Myles and their ranch hand Hank trying to maintain the status quo. Levi had some changes he'd like to institute to make things a bit easier, as well as possibly more profitable, but so far his silent partners—his other three brothers—were either AWOL or kept voting to maintain things as they were.

"What brings you into town?" Mrs. Fisher asked, leaning her hip against the counter.

"Coffee." He lifted the cup to his lips. It wasn't as strong as the brew he sipped at the pasture fence each dawn, but at least he hadn't had to make it.

"Either of y'all want breakfast?" She waggled a finger at Jackie and Levi.

Jackie shook her head and Levi shrugged, undecided. Jackie had been quiet so far, but the fact that she wasn't ordering anything suggested she might be tracking him specifically. In other words, she'd spotted the ranch's truck and had come in to see if today was the day a Wylder accepted her advances. He was fairly certain he wasn't her first pick, and personally, he was holding out for a woman who thought of him and nobody else.

If he ordered a meal he couldn't escape.

"You're wasting away," Mrs. Fisher said to Levi. "I heard you boys haven't been eating right since your mama left the ranch."

He bristled as the woman to his right gave him an amused, darting glance. It was true that everyone on the ranch had tightened their belts a notch since his mom had moved to town several months ago, but they weren't completely inept. He could grill a fine steak, and Myles was pretty good at making waffles.

"You need a woman to fatten you up," Jackie said. Her long fingers curled around his biceps.

"It's fine. I'm fine." He pushed himself off his stool and placed his hat on his head. "Was just in town for a radiator hose and thought I'd stop by and say hello." He dropped a few bills on the counter for his coffee.

"You paid for it, so might as well drink it." Mrs. Fisher topped up his cup.

He tipped it back and took a long slurp. Man, that was hot. He set it down, half-empty. "Gimme a muffin to go."

Mrs. Fisher whipped the tea towel out of her checkered apron, whacking him. "Mind your manners or I'll have your ear."

Chagrined, he sat again. "Please."

"Take off your hat if you're sitting at my counter," she chided. He obeyed.

"Are you going to Friday's game?" Jackie asked.

He never missed one if he could help it, and she knew it.

"We'll see."

"I'll save you a seat." He caught her eyeing the woman to his right. "I'm Jackie Moorhouse," she said to her. Jackie reached past him to shake hands, pressing her chest against his shoulder.

"Laura Oakes," the newcomer replied. She had a gentle voice that was lacking the typical Texas drawl commonly heard in Sweetheart Creek.

"You look familiar," Jackie said. "Did you win Miss Texas?"

She shook her head.

"Rodeo queen in San Antonio?"

Another shake of her head. Levi sized her up. There was that hint of familiarity about her, that was for sure.

"Riverbend pageant?"

Mrs. Fisher interrupted the questioning by placing a blueberry muffin in front of Levi, just the way he liked it: heated for a few seconds in the microwave and served with a pat of butter. It wasn't packaged to go, but there was no point arguing. Especially when he'd apparently left his manners back at the ranch.

"Thanks."

Mrs. Fisher gestured to the woman who looked like she'd stepped out of a magazine, saying, "Levi, you remember Laura?"

"Can't say I do," he admitted. "Car break down while passing through?" He stuffed half the muffin in his mouth.

A shadow passed over the stranger's face as he gazed at her. There was a tickle in the back of his mind, and a twist in his gut.

"It'll start again soon."

The way she jutted out her chin, as if daring him to impeach her independence, hit him with a jolt. A memory popped up in his mind, as bright and vivid as if it had happened only a minute before rather than a dozen summers ago.

"Laura," he said, turning to face her more fully, cataloguing the changes. They were boggling. "You're Laura."

She gave a sidelong glance toward the door, as though she might want to escape.

"You used to come into the hardware store." He felt himself smiling at the memory. She was someone's niece or something like that. Who had she been staying with? She'd been in town for part of the summer when he'd been fifteen and working his first job off the ranch, as dictated by his father. She would come into the shop, her hair wild, her nose covered in freckles, her clothes a bit too short, as though she'd just gone through a major growth spurt, and she'd ask him a million questions about how to fix something. Each time she'd left he'd had a feeling of things left unsaid. It was the oddest feeling, one he'd never figured out.

Once he'd asked if she needed help, and he'd gotten that same chin tilt he'd received a minute ago. It had quickly become a game for him, to see if he could get her to do that each time she came in. She was so determined to be independent, and he'd admired her ability to take on projects most thirteen-year-olds wouldn't have. He'd often wondered what had happened to her.

Apparently she'd grown up and become gorgeous.

"You do remember!" Mrs. Fisher said, her hands clasped near the sparkly fringe of her shirt.

"What?" Jackie asked, tipping forward against the counter. "Remember what?"

"Maybe you could show her around town," Mrs. Fisher suggested to Levi.

"Sorry. Busy." He shoved the last of his muffin in his mouth. Laura was gorgeous and he'd admired her perseverance back then, but lately the ranch was just problem after problem and it was grinding him down. He didn't have time to play tour guide.

"Levi!" the older woman snapped. "Your mother will have your ear for being so unwelcoming."

"I can show Laura around, Mrs. Fisher," Jackie offered.

Levi gave her a grateful smile and stood. As he fished more money out of his wallet he took a cautious step back, in case Mrs. Fisher decided to act as his mother's proxy and take his ear in a tight grip.

"How long are you in town for?" Jackie asked Laura, and Levi found himself waiting for her answer, which was a shrug that made her sleeveless purple sundress shift along her shoulder. How did her red nail polish and lipstick look so…*vibrant* with her purple dress?

"A few weeks for sure. Possibly longer." There was a question in her last statement, as though she might be asking if she was welcome to stay.

"I was thinking Levi would be a great guide," Mrs. Fisher stated, and he found himself nodding before he caught himself. She added, "You're busy, Jackie."

"*I'm* busy," Levi protested, his neck prickling with heat when Laura gave him a silent, knowing look.

"Levi…" the waitress murmured in warning.

"I'm not a tour guide, Mrs. Fisher. I have a ranch to run. If my brothers would step in and free up my time I'd be more than happy to show Laura around."

"Then show her the ranch," she replied. "Wouldn't that be fun, Laura? Do you still like horses?"

"I think she outgrew that phase," Levi said kindly, trying to give the woman an out. "Anyway, her nails wouldn't last a second on the ranch. Don't inflict that upon her manicure. I hear they're expensive."

Laura stood, slinging her purse strap onto her shoulder. "He's right. We're both busy. I have things to attend to, and I don't belong on a ranch with these nails." She slapped her debit card onto the counter. "Thank you for thinking of me, though, Mrs. Fisher."

Levi swallowed. "I'm sorry. I didn't mean to offend."

"No offense taken." Her tone was slightly cool, and he felt as though he should spend a bit more time getting off the ranch to practice his social skills.

"Hon, this here is Luanne's grandniece," Mrs. Fisher said pointedly.

Levi closed his eyes for a second, trying to remember the news from last summer around Luanne's passing. Her home had been left to her grandniece, the model. And, more recently, the news was that she was coming to town to take care of Luanne's home and possessions.

Laura.

"Sorry for your loss," he said, his stomach giving a strange jolt as her beautiful, sad eyes met his. He gave a polite nod, then made his way out of the diner before he acted any worse toward the poor woman than he already had.

***

LAURA HAD NEVER in her entire life been so relieved to be handed a key. She'd barely thanked Nina, who had arrived shortly after Levi cleared out, before she'd scuttled out of the diner in turn. He had obviously been assuming, and thus avoiding, a setup between the two of them, and had judged her for her appearance rather than for herself.

His attitude made his good looks a downright waste.

Not that she was looking for a man right now. She was here

to figure out where to go next with the name she'd made for herself. Create her own perfume line? Start a nonprofit for teens who needed help? Fall in love and get married? Start a travel blog? Or something she hadn't thought of yet. That's why she was here.

She stormed down Main Street, frustrated with her feelings, glancing in the hardware store window out of habit. Where had that kind, patient teenage version of Levi gone? How had he grown up into someone so abrupt? She'd come up with so many excuses to go in and buy something from him, and he'd seemed so delighted to help her find the right size bolt, deal with skunks without getting herself sprayed, or teach her how to choose the right stain for the fence. And even though he'd challenged her independence at times with his tempting offers to help, he'd become someone she could count on to not judge her if her projects went awry, or to patiently run through his instructions once again, nothing but kindness in his steady, blue-eyed gaze.

She caught her reflection in the store window and jolted. Instead of the frizzy-haired, skinny girl she'd been as a teen, there was a stately, slender woman. She was wearing a bright dress, high heels, and had a tan that couldn't be real due to its uniform perfection. Her hair was a thing of beauty, her makeup exquisite, her eyebrows meticulously tweezed, her lashes enviously long. It was apparent she didn't fit in around here, and didn't belong on a ranch. Levi hadn't been wrong to judge her.

She walked faster as emotions ran through her. The summer she'd spent here had felt like a turning point. She had arrived feeling lost and broken, and had left feeling strong and capable of achieving any goals she set for herself. She had felt as though she had the power to make something of her life, but what had she done? She had taken that hopeful girl and turned her into something fake, once again lost and feeling alone.

Sweat prickled along her spine and her eyes burned.

She would not cry. Not here. Not now.

She had done good things with her fame and generous income. She had helped support animal shelters, built water wells in impoverished areas of the world, and taught inner city adults to read. She was more than the delicate flower Levi had assumed she was.

Head high. Chin up.

By the time she made it to her car at that blistering pace, she was sweating. The armadillo was nowhere to be seen, and she closed her eyes, still squeezing the key to Luanne's house in her hand.

Should she rescue her suitcase first, or see if her car would start? She turned to look back into town, past the used car lot she hadn't even noticed earlier on her run from Bill, the armadillo. A man was standing in front of the small building, the triangular flags above the short row of cars flapping in a gust of wind. He was watching her, hands on his hips. Feeling as though she needed to act as though she knew what she was doing, Laura ducked into her car first to see if it would start.

It wouldn't. She checked the time. It had been far more than twenty minutes. What was its deal?

Laura stepped out of the Beetle and scanned the dry grass along the road. Where was her suitcase? Hadn't it slid in just about there?

A truck slowed beside her, and she glanced up, surprised to see Levi driving the faded old pickup she'd seen in front of the Longhorn.

He stopped, windows down, the dark brown hair around his ears fluttering in the breeze as though he'd put off getting a haircut for too long. He adjusted his cowboy hat over his forehead as if he might be thinking before speaking. Not a bad trait. It was unfortunate he hadn't utilized it earlier.

"I'd like to apologize for back there," he said with great care. "If you find you want a tour of town, I can do that. I'll warn you, though, I spend most of my time on the family ranch or at the field watching football." He looked like he had more to say, but instead closed his mouth. Another good trait. He knew when to stop talking.

He studied her car with interest for another moment. "Won't start?"

She shook her head. "Usually it only needs twenty minutes."

"Can I give you a ride somewhere?"

"As a matter of fact, you can." She marched to the passenger side of his truck, intent on making him do a good deed in order to make amends. Or maybe just to somehow prove she was more than whatever he thought he'd seen in her at the diner. She yanked open the creaky door.

"Sorry, it doesn't get used much. The dog usually hops in from this side."

She hoisted herself up onto the springy seat, displacing a layer of dust that made her nose tickle. She sneezed.

"Bless you."

"Thank you."

He put the truck in gear. "To Luanne's, I presume?"

"Yes. Do you know the address?" She mentally crossed her fingers, realizing that unless they took her old meandering bike route to Luanne's she might not be able to find it on the first try.

"I don't. But I do know how to get there." His lips quirked as if he was holding back a smile. He was cute when he did that. Too cute. Like when he'd been a teenager.

"Good." She sat stiffly as he began driving, lifting his fingers off the steering wheel in a casual wave to an oncoming truck pulling a horse trailer. The other driver's interest was focused on her, Laura noted.

The window was still down and the wind tangled her hair as they picked up speed. She looked for a button, but it was a crank style.

When she reached for it, Levi said in a gentle, yet warning

tone, "I leave the windows down as they don't always go back up. And if they do, they don't always come down again. No AC."

"Why don't you fix them?"

He shrugged. "It's old. This isn't the ranch's going-to-town truck."

"But you went to town in it."

"Yup."

The town that was growing smaller behind them.

"Luanne lives in town," she said sharply, panic setting in. Just because Sweetheart Creek was small, it didn't mean she should assume it was safe.

"Just going to turn the truck around up here," he explained, pointing to a pullout that allowed access to a pasture just beyond the sign that said Thank You for Visiting Sweetheart Creek. Below, someone had tacked on another sign that said Go Torpedoes!

When he'd turned the truck around as promised, they headed back in the direction of her car. Near where they'd passed the horse trailer, in the ditch opposite her VW, several boys had parked their bicycles and were standing in a circle. One waved something small and dainty in the air.

Laura sat up, her stomach dropping. "My suitcase."

There was a flash of red fabric, then a scrap of something lacy as another boy found a trophy. She covered her mouth in horror. They were waving her lingerie around like a prize. Her very sexy, very expensive, very personal lingerie.

Levi pulled over just as Laura sank down in her seat, whispering, "Keep going! Keep going!"

He ignored her, hopping out, his shoulders broad, his stance saying he meant business as he addressed the boys. Laura tentatively opened her door, sliding out onto the soft dirt at the edge of the road. Her heels sank in and she lost her balance, wavering for one brief second before gravity ruthlessly sent her tumbling into the ditch, skinning her knees and palms in the loose gravel and dry grass as she let out an embarrassing squeak of surprise.

"Whoa." Levi was there in a flash, holding her elbow as he helped her up.

Laura dusted herself off, wishing she had superpowers. Namely ones that would make her invisible. She caught sight of what Levi was holding in his free hand. It was a week's worth of delicate lace, and she debated whether fainting would save her from experiencing the full brunt of this mortifying moment. Her favorite suitcase, one that had traveled the world with her, was split at the seams, spilling her personal items for all to see.

Levi gave her elbow a small squeeze. "You doing all right there?"

She forced her head to move up and down, when all she wanted to do was shake it and sit down and cry at how everything felt as though it was piling up on her today.

The boys had cycled a short way down the road, stopping at a safe distance to call out something she couldn't hear. Levi, jaw set, collected her clothing with efficient moves, cradling the split case, then placing it in the back of his pickup. If he drove fast enough into town she was pretty sure all her newly retrieved undergarments would be blown out, strewn about like freebies in a small town parade sponsored by La Perla.

Laura hadn't moved from her spot at the bottom of the ditch, and from behind her, Levi asked, "Got yourself stuck down there?"

She looked down at her feet, at her fitted dress, then turned to survey the unforgiving incline. She was everything he'd judged her to be earlier, and it was beyond humbling.

Levi began moving toward her again, and she pointed a finger at him. "Don't you dare pick me up and carry me like a useless female."

There must've been something in her tone because he halted abruptly, hands raised in surrender.

She eyed the slope to the truck. There was only one way to make it up with any dignity and grace. She was going to have to go barefoot. She bent to undo the straps of her shoes, ignoring how torn up her knees were. The grass in the ditch was prickly, dry and similar to fierce little swords. Walking over it would surely hurt worse than having the more tender areas of her body waxed for a bikini shoot. But she was not going to flail about in these heels, and she was not going to accept being helpless.

She glanced at the sky while trying to slip off one dusty red Jimmy Choo. Cloudless. No chance of a freak lightning strike. She wobbled dangerously.

"I'm sorry," she said in a smooth voice, reaching out and indicating she'd like to use Levi to support her. "Would you be able to assist me?"

He came down the embankment once more, angling his feet so the heels of his boots dug into the ground, then tilted his shoulder her way. The man was tall, even taller than she was. "You sure I can't just hoist you into the truck like a sack of potatoes?"

She had been avoiding looking at him as she placed a hand on his warm shoulder, but now snapped a glance at him, finding amusement twinkling in his cloudless blue eyes.

"You think this is funny?"

"Don't you?"

"I hate feeling helpless."

Anger tore through her like a windstorm at how she'd allowed her life to veer off the tracks. She was a washed up model with no solid new career ideas, despite having known this day was coming. She'd recently dumped a man she should have released into the dating wilds years ago, and was currently stuck in a ditch because she had chosen to wear heels that were way out of place in this town. She'd dressed like this to show off, but all she'd done was reveal what a princess she'd become.

Her frustration bubbled over and she grumbled, "I hate these shoes. I hate my nails. I hate my eyelashes. I hate my highlights. I hate this dress and I hate my fake tan. And I could really use a second milkshake right now."

Levi studied her for a moment, then said, "I like your dress."

She gave him a pitiful look and they burst out laughing.

"Looks like you may have hit rock bottom there." He was cuter when he smiled, and his drawl was dead to rights the sexiest thing she'd heard in eons. Maybe his good looks weren't a complete and utter waste, after all.

"This isn't rock bottom," she whispered, her lip trembling dangerously. "Trust me." But it felt pretty darn close.

"I know." There was nothing but kindness and understanding in his tired eyes. How did a man this young seem so old in this moment, as if the world was weighing on him like it was on her?

She let out a long sigh of defeat. It was difficult to fight the truth sometimes. But that was why she was here, right? Figure things out. Decide what she did and didn't want in her life moving forward.

Laura gasped as Levi lifted her into the air, one arm behind her legs and the other around her waist, in a quick move she didn't have time to protest. In seconds he had her up the hill and into the passenger seat, her loosened shoe slipping off her foot in the process. His arms felt strong, his body capable. Before she could say thank-you, he had turned away to retrieve her shoe.

He handed it to her. "Cinderella."

"I'm not a princess," she muttered.

"You said that years ago, with that same jut of your chin." His smile was kind and caused a swarm of butterflies to flutter in her stomach.

"Did I?"

"In the hardware store."

"Why were you working there? Aren't you a cowboy with a ranch or something?" She'd always wondered that. He had obviously been a cowboy, and still was.

"I am," he admitted. "My dad insisted we all experience life off of the ranch, as well as learn to work for someone who wasn't family. I think it was meant to make us appreciate the ranch more."

"Did it work?"

"He scored forty."

"What does that mean?"

"Forty percent. Two of his five sons stayed on the ranch."

The skin around his mouth pinched. There was a story there, and a part of her hoped she stayed in Sweetheart Creek long enough to find out what it was.

3

---

*B*ack on the ranch, Levi parked his Chevy behind the barn that served as a riding stable, tucking the key in the visor before getting out. Seeing the manager's pickup, he whistled while ambling inside to say good morning, his good deed of the day accomplished by giving Laura a ride to her aunt's house, then giving her Clint's number so she could get him to tow her car to his shop and take a peek at it. Levi couldn't recall feeling this upbeat in weeks. Going to town had been a good decision. He should make a point of leaving the ranch more often.

Laura hadn't allowed him to fix up her knees, though, which had taken a beating from her tumble into the ditch, and Levi felt bad for the way her problems seemed to be piling up on her. At least he'd felt as though he'd redeemed himself in regards to his earlier crankiness. Then again, if he'd stayed home he would probably still be ahead. But he wouldn't have bumped into her, and that had been nice.

The stable's small rear door opened on well-oiled hinges, and he hollered a hello so as not to startle the woman in charge of the ranch's riding program. The place was darker than usual, and he found it odd that Betty hadn't yet propped open the large doors to the ring. Riders would be arriving soon, and she was always prepared. Which meant something was up.

The riding program, a side business within the ranch, helped children with special needs, and had been doing so ever since he'd been a kid, continuing his grandmother's legacy. Monitored rides around the ring helped kids of all ages cope with anxiety, anger, and even some physical issues, in ways that astounded him to this day.

"That you, Levi?" Betty called. "I was hoping to have a chance to chat."

The matronly cowgirl stepped out of her office, her checkered Western blouse spilling over the waistband of her broken-in jeans.

"What's on your mind?" he asked, as they moved into her office.

"I've got some bad news."

"Oh?" Levi leaned against the doorjamb. Betty wasn't one to mince words, and while he appreciated her directness, he cringed to think what kind of bad news she was about to deliver.

She drew in a long breath.

"Lame horse?" he offered.

"I'm needed in California."

Levi felt the air leave his lungs as he sank into a faded, dusty armchair near the door. He plucked his cowboy hat from his head and pushed his fingers through his hair as though hoping the action would loosen his thoughts, help him problem-solve running a riding arena, which only Betty knew how to do.

His dad had remarried three months ago, leaving Levi, the eldest, in charge of Sweet Meadows Ranch while he moved into town with his new bride, Sophia. Levi's brothers were supposed to come back to help him figure things out, but so far it was just him and Myles taking up the reins. Their granddad sometimes helped, but running this program would be too much for the retired seventy-nine-year-old.

And if he took care of it himself, it wouldn't be long before he found himself drowning due to the added, unfamiliar tasks. Could he find the funds to hire more help?

"How soon?" he asked.

"Immediately. Janet's husband was in a car accident," Betty said, referring to her son-in-law.

Levi's head jerked up, but not due to the familiar, faint pang at hearing his ex-girlfriend's name. "Is he okay? How are Janet and the kids?"

"Holding up, but it doesn't sound as though recovery is going to be swift or easy for Jason."

"She needs you," Levi said simply, standing while donning his hat. There was no conversation to be had. Betty had to go. Her family needed her. "Do you have enough for a flight?"

Betty gave him a warm hug. "You're just like your father—the best boss a woman could ask for."

"You're your own boss, and we both know it."

She released him, then grasped his forearms. "I've booked a flight for this afternoon, and while I hate to say it, I don't know when I'll be back. It could be as long as three months." There was a slight waver in her voice, and Levi knew the accident had been worse than he'd assumed. Either that or she really hated leaving him high and dry. Knowing Betty, it was probably a mix of both.

"We'll manage. What do you need?" He was already moving, ushering her toward her truck. He'd find someone. The riding program was secondary to her family's needs right now.

"I think I'm set, but what *you* need is someone who knows about riding stables. Someone who knows about kids with special needs. You can't have just anyone come in and place these vulnerable children on a mare." She stopped walking, pressing a strong hand against his forearm as she enunciated the next three words. "Hire someone good."

Levi adjusted his hat and cleared his throat. It was going to be impossible to replace Betty.

"I spent most of the night getting everything organized. Anyone smart will see what I've been doing and step in without missing a beat."

"How come I didn't see the light on in your office this morning? Or see your truck?"

He'd been out at the fence at dawn, in his usual thinking spot, his cup of coffee in hand.

She gave a tired smile. "We only see what we're looking for, Levi."

"Look at you, being all philosophical."

"Learn that lesson, hon. It'll serve you well." She returned to business mode. "The schedule is on the bulletin board, list of contacts in the filing cabinet. And while you were busy rejecting the chance to be a nice, welcoming fellow with Luanne's grandniece at the diner, I called today's riders and canceled as many as I could. But you still have three kids coming midafternoon." She raised a brow in reprimand for how he'd treated Laura.

He tipped his head so the brim of his hat would hide his sheepishness. Giving Laura a ride home no longer appeased the guilt he felt for the way he'd voiced his assumptions based on her appearance. But she did fall down a ditch in those heels, and the way she was all done up wasn't a good match for ranching life. He stood by that, and he felt she did, too, based on her little rant about her appearance. He had to admit, though, that it had been nice carrying her up the slope like that. She'd been soft, strong, warm, everything. Smelled good, too.

"I gave her a ride to Luanne's."

He'd wanted to stay, tend to her scrapes, maybe give her a kiss.

He was unfit for going out in public, wasn't he? The wrong woman falls down in front of him and he starts thinking and acting like he's infatuated. He was not looking to add a woman to his life. He didn't have time for that.

"Be *nice* to her. She's mourning."

"She can hold her own." He thought of how fiercely determined she'd been as a teen to exert her independence in the DIY arena. "She's not a delicate flower."

Although some parts of her were delicate, he supposed. His mind drifted to the itty-bitty bits of soft lace he'd taken from the boys when she'd tumbled into the ditch.

"Levi? Are you listening?"

"Yes, ma'am."

"I wrote everything down." Betty patted his cheek and shook her head at him. "It's a good thing you're a problem solver."

"What does that mean?"

"Other than the three riders coming this afternoon, you have a forty-eight hour window to figure things out," she said, turning to her pickup.

Today was Saturday, which meant he had the rest of today—after the three riders left—and tomorrow, since none came on Sundays. He had planned to spend the weekend out in the back forty with his brother Brant, the veterinarian, inspecting several hundred cows that should be pregnant. That was where the ranch made its bread and butter. And it saved on vet bills, having his brother go with him to check, since he didn't charge for his expertise, and billed wholesale for any veterinarian supplies they might need. Not many ranches had those perks.

"Can I pause the program for a week?" he asked.

"Those kids need this place." Betty's look was firm as she pulled him into a brief hug.

Her eyes were damp as she climbed into her truck. Levi closed her door, speaking through the window after she put it down. "Say hi to Janet and the family, and let us know if you need anything. We may be over a thousand miles away, but that doesn't mean we aren't standing right behind you."

Her eyes grew glassy for a brief second before she reached through the window to grip his jaw, giving it a gentle shake. "Don't let just anyone step into that stable, or you'll have your grandmother rolling over in her grave. She's the type who would haunt you, honey."

Levi chuckled. His grandmother Ruth had been a live wire all right, keeping everyone in line, from her husband, who still lived on the ranch, to half the town.

"I'm pretty sure you'd deal with me before I allowed things to fall apart in that ring."

Betty gave him a knowing smile. "I left you a list of people you might want to ask to step in for me, but they're all long shots when it comes to putting their lives on hold."

"I'll find someone."

The only problem was, kind of like trying to get the AWOL Cole, the second-born Wylder, to return home, Levi wasn't sure how he was going to do it, only that it was on him to accomplish it.

LAURA HAD CLOSED the door behind Levi after he'd carried her broken suitcase into the house over an hour ago, and she was still thinking about him—and not just because he was a rarity and seemed to match her in height, at nearly six foot four when wearing heels. He'd asked if she had a first aid kit for her scraped knees, and she'd assured him she did, eager to get him out of her aunt's house before she did anything rash, such as renew her old crush on him.

But instead of leaving, Levi had cemented his feet in the entry and announced that she needed to get Clint, the local mechanic, to take care of her car. So she'd found herself making the call to get it towed.

All the while Levi had been in the house, making sure she was set with all she might need, Laura had found herself wishing that he'd kiss her, which was the most puzzling part of her entire day. She was an adult. She shouldn't feel this level of desire to have him notice her—the real her—and be attracted to her as a result.

She was obviously still on the rebound from her breakup with Memphis, because she and Levi weren't a match for each other, and he'd made it clear he agreed.

But she was grateful for how, despite how busy he'd claimed to be, he had taken the time to look out for her, predicting what she might need and ensuring she had it before trucking off home. It had been reassuring and comforting, and had made her realize that attentive care was missing from her social circle back home. Nobody but her stepsister had fussed over or worried about her when she'd ended her career or broken up with her boyfriend of several years. But Levi had fussed over something as minor as skinned knees and a very old car. And it wasn't because he thought she was an incompetent princess, either.

Feeling unsettled by his care and attention, Laura headed to the kitchen and pulled her water bottle and paperback from her purse, easing the load in her designer handbag before going back to store it in the hall closet.

Levi wasn't worth thinking about. It was just small-town hospitality kicking in. She was here to take care of her aunt's things, get the house ready for sale, while sorting out her next career and life moves. After which she'd head back to New York, if that's where she needed to be.

She returned to the kitchen and dug her phone out from the pages of her paperback, where it had snugged itself, then checked her emails. There was one from her agent, a drafted contract for her to look over in regards to starting her own perfume line. Laura set down her phone, vowing to read through it after supper, when she could concentrate better.

Hands on her hips, she surveyed the familiar house. It still smelled like her aunt's hair spray. Laura could practically see her thirteen-year-old self running in with bare feet, grass in her hair from sprawling on the lawn to daydream, or from roaming through the neighborhood or wading in Sweetheart Creek with the other kids.

She had been horse crazy back then, and Nina had allowed her to come ride on her family's small acreage a few times a week. She didn't have many chances to ride in New York as an adult, but occasionally she'd treat herself to a carriage ride through Central Park, even though it wasn't the same thing. There was something about hearing the clack of hooves and being surrounded by nature that took her heart rate down to normal and reestablished her priorities.

In the kitchen she aimlessly opened a few cupboards and drawers. Half-empty boxes of cereal, bags of chocolate chips, partially consumed jars of condiments, twist ties, dishes, tablecloths. What was she supposed to do with everything? Sell the house as it was, fully furnished and stocked? How could she hand her aunt's entire life and personal items over to a stranger? What if there were journals tucked away somewhere that would go undiscovered until someone emptied the place?

Laura opened a drawer, which squeaked. She pulled out an eggbeater with a wooden crank that connected to a metal gear. She had loved helping her aunt make French toast in the mornings, using this beater to whip the eggs. She laid it on the counter, starting a pile of things she would take home with her.

But what about the measuring cups and spoons, mixing bowls and cookie sheets? It was going to take forever to find a worthy home for everything. Luanne had provided a haven for her the summer her parents had split up, and the remnants of her great-aunt's life deserved so much more than to be divided, given away or sold at auction.

Laura walked into the living room, thinking it might be easier to deal with, less full of memories. There she was faced with shelves of movies, books and figurines, needlepoint and family portraits.

She sat heavily in the recliner facing a large flat-screen TV, one quite sizable for a woman who mostly watched game shows. Was that the set she'd mentioned winning at a football game fundraiser last year?

The table beside the chair was stacked with murder mysteries and a basket of knitting supplies. This room wasn't going to be any easier to handle.

Marching back into the kitchen, Laura opened the fridge freezer. There, among the margarine containers with masking tape labels declaring soup stocks and leftovers, was a pint of her favorite ice cream. Triple chocolate caramel swirl, with walnuts and marshmallows. It was as though her aunt had selected it for her, placing it at the front of the freezer, knowing Laura would need its comfort.

She pulled it out and scooped herself a bowl, then went to sit on the front steps in the midday heat to think. It wasn't long before the casserole parade started, neighbors coming by with "a little something to tide her over." Laura protested at first, stating she was only one person, but quickly learned that "no" was not an answer they wanted to hear in response to their small town hospitality.

And it was then that she realized what she could do to thank Levi for making her feel welcome and cared for, even though it hadn't been his first choice that morning.

LEVI HAD CALLED everyone on Betty's list, without success. Folks had offered to lend a hand in the riding arena here and there, but it was too much to ask any volunteer to stay as long as he required. He needed to hire someone. Someone other than his grandfather, Carmichael, who was currently sitting on a hay bale near him in the stable, grumbling and insisting that he *was* helping out.

Levi supposed he should go easy on the man, even though he hadn't needed the running commentary on how to saddle a horse. Granddad was trying to be helpful, and his aging body didn't allow him to do all the things he once had without thought. And it was true that Levi had indeed forgotten that Rose liked to sidestep into the person saddling her, making the heads-up appreciated.

Betty had given Levi too much credit, and in approximately fifteen minutes he was going to have to figure out how to do all the things she did for the Sweet Meadows Ranch riders. He figured he'd be extra careful, put each rider on their favorite horse of the bunch, lead them around the ring, and all would be good. Right? Was there more to it than that?

Half an hour later Levi was wiping the sweat from his brow and wondering how Betty did it all. Everyone was on their mount of choice—after frantically saddling up new ones, as he'd selected the wrong horses to begin with. But so far nobody had fallen off or thrown a temper tantrum, even though he felt as though the potential for a meltdown was currently stalking him from the periphery. The kids who had come this afternoon had been thrown when they'd discovered Betty was away. Levi didn't think their parents had ever been so hands-on before, as they normally enjoyed a glass of sweet tea from Betty's office fridge while sitting in the shade of a large oak near the stable doors during their child's forty-five-minute ride. Today they were in the ring, giving him constant pointers.

Levi knew horses.

He didn't know special-needs kids.

And he didn't know special-needs kids on horses.

When Betty returned she was getting a raise.

But then in the midst of the chaos, one of the children had smiled, and it had given him an instant insight as to why Betty did this every week. Those smiles were pure gold and he would do anything to get another one.

The problem was he had a ranch to run full-time, and he couldn't take care of this riding program six days a week, as well.

He propped himself against the railing of the arena to watch for a moment, Carmichael having long ago settled at the base of the nearby oak and tipped his hat down over his eyes. Levi's dog, Lupe, and Myles's dog, Buckey, were lying beside him, panting, watching the action in the ring.

There had to be a solution. Likely one sitting in front of him that he simply hadn't considered yet.

Levi felt a light hand on his shoulder and he jolted in surprise. He turned, knocking a dish to the ground.

Laura.

She crouched, quickly gathering up what appeared to be ginger cookies and placing them back on the plate, which luckily hadn't broken. She was wearing a different dress than she'd had on earlier, this one sun-yellow, with a skirt that fanned out about her long, slim legs as she squatted there. "Sorry. You startled me." Levi dropped beside her, grabbing the last cookie and taking a peek at her expression. She looked a bit emotionally beat up. "Plate's okay?"

"Seems to be."

He tipped forward, reaching to take it for her as she rose. The back of her head hit him square in the face, knocking his hat off and igniting some ricocheting fireworks in his vision. He clutched his nose as it started bleeding.

They both stood, dazed. Laura's hand was at the back of her head, her expression one of horror when she caught sight of his face.

"I am so sorry! Are you okay?"

"Fine." He didn't sound fine. His voice sounded funny. Had she broken his nose? It hurt like it might be.

One of the children, Bronwyn, was riding her horse along the fence line, going in large circles. She came up alongside, her eyes widening as she spied him and his nose. A shriek started low in her belly, growing louder until it pierced his eardrums. Her mom, holding the horse's lead, jumped in alarm and the horse shifted sideways, its head jerking back.

"Tighten the lead!" Levi shouted, and his dog immediately appeared at his heels, ready to herd if given the signal. Bronwyn's mom needed to slide her grip up toward the horse's snout, quickly and firmly, to keep Cherry under control in case the horse reacted to the human panic.

Levi stepped toward the railing, prepared to vault the nearly chest-high fence so he could grab the horse if it reared. The child screamed louder, letting go of Cherry's reins.

"Hold the reins, Bronwyn!"

He felt a none-too-gentle shove as Laura said, "You need to get out of here. You're making things worse."

This was *his* ranch, and he knew horses. He couldn't leave in the midst of a brewing crisis. He'd done that once and had nearly lost Ryan as a result.

Laura gave him another hard shove, then slipped between the railing's thick horizontal boards, stepping into the well-trod dirt of the arena in her delicate white shoes. Her cookies were scattered again, light brown discs in the green grass. Without hesitation, she reached past Bronwyn's mom, grabbing Cherry's bridle with her right hand, pulling down firmly while making shushing noises to the animal and child. Her left hand went to Bronwyn's knee in comfort, and Levi opened his mouth to issue a warning about the child's sensory issues. A stranger touching her would surely escalate Bronwyn's episode.

Levi was already halfway over the fence when he registered the cessation of screams. Bronwyn hadn't yanked her leg out of Laura's reach, inadvertently spurring Cherry. Instead, the startled child was listening to Laura and quickly calming down.

Levi eased himself back to the ground in awe, holding his

sleeve to his nose. He had vastly underestimated Laura Oakes, and for some reason that made him very happy.

LAURA STAYED in the riding arena until she was certain things were back under control. Then she moved to the edge, noting she'd ruined her satin ballet flats as well as her apology to Levi. The soft ginger cookies were now being eaten by a large, shaggy dog and a slightly larger, black one. Worried they would get sick from eating the sweet treats, she retrieved the plate and the last cookie from the grass.

A man moved in the shadows of the stable nearby, and she peered closer, realizing it was Levi, staying out of sight. He had propped himself in the doorway, looking very much the stereotypical cowboy. Rugged, handsome, that quiet control running like an underwater current.

An older cowboy, who walked like he'd spent too many years on a horse, joined Levi. The men's sentences were short, the shake of their heads frequent. When the older man finished talking to Levi, Laura headed his way, the two dogs following her.

"Thank you," Levi said, when she came within earshot.

"*This* was supposed to be a thank-you." She held up the plate with the one remaining cookie, plucking a piece of dried grass off it in the process.

Levi took the cookie and bit into it. His face registered surprise. "These are good. I can see why Lupe and Buckey tried to eat them all."

"I hope they don't make them sick."

"I doubt they will." Levi's focus was on the uneaten half of his cookie. "And anyway, they're ranch dogs. They spend most of their time outdoors, so if they get an upset stomach, they won't ruin the carpet."

The old cowboy had reappeared, appraising Laura. "Lupe eats just about anything." He jerked a thumb toward Levi, a hint of affection in his tone as he added, "Just like this one. That's probably why Brant chose him for Levi. They're the same mixed breed and love being on a ranch."

Levi, chewing the last of the cookie, gave a light snort of amusement, but didn't disagree.

"I'm Laura Oakes." She put out her hand, taking care to give the older cowboy a firm shake while meeting his eye.

"Carmichael. Sorry for your loss, my dear. Your aunt was a great woman."

"She was. Thank you."

"So what are you thanking Levi for?" Carmichael had crossed his arms and was studying her closely. "Because it looks to me like he should be doing the thanking."

"I hadn't gotten that far, Granddad."

"Levi gave me a ride this morning and made sure I was settled in at Aunt Luanne's," Laura said.

"Glad he could be of use," Carmichael said.

"He was, thank you." It felt awkward speaking about Levi as though he wasn't there, and Laura made a point of turning to him and repeating her thank-you, the clarity of his blue eyes once again stirring up that weird urge to kiss him. Would that old crush ever loosen its grip? She was a grown up now, and it was time to break that old habit of waiting and hoping for him to notice and care.

"And thank you for saving my wife's riding business back there." Carmichael said. "God rest her soul."

"I really didn't do anything. And...I'm sorry for *your* loss."

"It's been years now. She started this outreach program. Betty Coulter usually runs it, but she's away on a family emergency." Carmichael shot Levi a quick look that caused the younger cowboy to stiffen with awareness, as though he knew something was coming.

"Can I offer you a job in the ring?" Carmichael asked.

Laura was flattered. "Thank you, but I know nothing about this sort of thing." She couldn't help but glance at Levi, noting that he'd shucked the checkered, long-sleeved shirt he'd been wearing, and that his white T-shirt showed off some impressive chest muscles. "And I do have to get back to New York once I've finished taking care of my aunt's estate."

"Well, seems to me you have an instinct for horses and riders." The old man tipped his head to the right and raised his brows, challenging her to disagree. "I heard you have plenty of time to sort through your aunt's things."

"Granddad," Levi said gently.

She wanted to say she needed to hustle back to the city, but that was neither urgent nor her plan. In fact, she couldn't think of a single excuse as to why she might need to hurry back to the Big Apple. And she *had* planned to spend time sorting out her next step in life while here. But she really didn't need a job tying her down and distracting her. She glanced at Levi, noting how his nose seemed to be swelling. It looked awful and possibly broken.

"Is your nose okay?"

"It ain't broke," Carmichael said, not looking at his grandson.

"It looks like it's…not good."

"We'd be much obliged if you could find it in your heart to step in for a few days," Carmichael said. "That is, until Levi's able to hire someone a little more permanent. After all, he can't find someone like you in one day, and you can't clean a lifetime out of a house in one day, either."

He was good, she'd give him that.

"Tomorrow's Sunday, so there's no riding," Carmichael said casually, "but how about we see you Monday morning at nine. Stop by for coffee and we'll see where you're at with things. And if you need help with the house, you let me know. I had to go through Ruth's belongings and that was darn near the hardest thing I ever did. Don't you go rushing something like that. You don't want regrets around a loved one's death."

His dark brown eyes were open, honest, and so sincere it was all she could do not to cry. Laura nodded, unable to use her voice, much less refuse his Monday morning offer.

The only question in her mind was whether she would decide to come out and give it a try, and whether Levi would mind.

4

Levi and his granddad had argued for two days over bringing Laura in to help with the riding program. So far, Carmichael was winning.

"I'll admit it would be nice to hand the problem off to someone," Levi said, whacking a nail into the board Carmichael was holding against the fence out by the barn. "But I need someone who can handle all of it. I have work to do, and she's admitted she doesn't know much about ranches."

"She won't be a problem," Carmichael said. "She calmed that horse and that little girl in one quick move. She's a gentle soul and that's what matters most when you're dealing with horses and kids."

Next, his grandfather would be labeling Laura a horse whisperer.

"It doesn't mean she's the right person," Levi protested, knowing he was wasting his energy arguing against the inevitable. And he had to admit he'd been impressed with how Laura had averted a possible disaster on Saturday.

"Then I guess we'll see in an hour, won't we?" Carmichael said.

"If she shows up."

"She's not in a hurry to go home. I can tell. Clint said she had her car packed to the gills, like she plans on sticking around some."

"She's a city girl, Granddad."

"A model by trade, I hear. With the face and figure to back up the claim."

Finished fixing the railing, Levi turned to his grandfather. "Exactly. She hardly has the résumé of someone you should be entrusting Grandma's passion project to. It's not just a safety issue, but a question of the ranch's reputation."

Carmichael frowned, his eyes growing stormy. "You think I haven't considered all that? My gut says this is right."

His grandfather's gut never failed, even when logic added up against it.

"Anyway, you have a better idea?" he asked, his wrinkled tanned face creasing into a smile.

"You know I don't."

"If it's not her, then we shut it down."

"Shut down the riding program?" That was unexpected.

"You heard me. Anyway, what's the worst she could do?"

That was the unknown that kept Levi's mind going in circles, and he feared it could be plenty. He picked up the tools and headed to the machine shed, a building large enough to hold several tractors as well as his mother's no-longer-running Mustang. Carmichael began ambling in the direction of his little place, beyond a hedge of holly trees that separated it from the main house.

Levi checked his watch. It was almost nine, which meant it was time for Carmichael's second breakfast—a candy bar—and a treat for his little dog Missy. That also meant Carmichael likely had no plans to chat with Laura, should she arrive. He liked to savor every morsel of his candy bars, and he didn't share.

Levi went on to the ranch house, found his blue, whitespecked enamel camping cup from earlier and, topped it up with coffee, then grabbed a dog biscuit and stepped out onto the long wraparound porch. Lupe was waiting for him, knowing the routine of sunrise with coffee, a few hours work, then a coffee on the porch, along with a doggy biscuit for him if the day warranted time for a break. He took his biscuit to his spot at the top of the steps and lay down to eat.

If Laura did show up, what would she be wearing? Something designer and impractical, like she had when she'd arrived in town on Saturday?

Levi rubbed his still-sore nose, grateful he hadn't gotten two black eyes out of their collision. That would be a fun one to explain around town.

What if she turned up in a pair of Wranglers that hugged her bottom? He was a sucker for a tall woman in a tight pair of jeans. And he had to admit that the designers who made Wranglers knew what they were doing. Nothing accented a woman's figure and strong thighs like their denim collection did. If Laura showed up in the right gear he had a feeling he would be a lost cause, despite his plans to avoid getting tied up in a distraction before the ranch management issue was settled among the brothers.

Levi paced the porch, his coffee still untouched, trying to think about anything but Laura, which proved to be an exercise in futility. By the time the old grandfather clock chimed from inside the house, the day was already hinting at the heat they'd have by midafternoon. Shortly after the clock stopped bonging Luanne's old Mercury rolled into the yard, bringing Buckey, Myles's Rottweiler-and-lab mix, out of the shade to bark a warning.

Laura had come.

Levi went to meet the car, after sending Buckey back to the shade of the nearby hedge, tail wagging. The car door opened with a dry creak, and a long blue-jeaned leg stretched out, a very new looking blue cowboy boot hitting the ground. Those feet would have blisters by sundown.

"Good morning," he said, joining her, coffee in hand. He held the car door for her, even though there was no risk of it closing. Lupe nosed in on her, sniffing around like he expected cookies. Laura gave him a few pats before the dog returned to Levi's side.

"Good morning," she said, her voice sweet and happy.

"Came for a chat and coffee?" Levi asked.

Carmichael, as predicted, was nowhere to be seen.

Before Levi could react, Laura thanked him, took his cup and lifted it to her dark pink lips. He stood there with his mouth open as she took a sip, a twinkle playing in her hazel eyes. She handed back the now lipstick-stained cup and he stared at it, completely at a loss over how he should react to this beautiful woman claiming something that had been against his lips only moments ago.

She snugged a Yankees ball cap low on her forehead and gave a quick nod. "I thought about it, and my answer is yes. I need a distraction from dealing with the house."

"You're here to help?"

"If you still need it."

Judging by the thundering in his ears, Levi needed more than that.

FOR THE PAST half an hour Laura had followed Levi around the stable as he introduced her to the horses, their personalities and the equipment she'd need to run the riding program. The red barn that served as the riding stable housed fifteen horses in the stalls along the north wall, and Levi spoke of each animal as if it was a good friend. The most intriguing part, however, had been the way he'd relaxed around them, and she'd caught more than just a glimpse of that teen she'd crushed on all those years ago.

She also understood why he'd blown her off, along with Mrs. Fisher's suggestion of a town and ranch tour. He had a lot going on. Even just an hour of his time had come with several interruptions. He had been phoned, texted, and hollered at from the stable doorway. This man didn't need more problems to solve. He needed them taken away, so he'd have time to relax and breathe.

And that was what she would do. Not just steal a big sip of his coffee to see how he'd react; she would help remove some problems from his plate and engage him in some lighthearted fun.

"When do the riders arrive?" she asked, as they saddled horses.

"In about half an hour." He addressed the ranch hand who had appeared in the doorway. "This about the well, Hank?"

The man nodded.

"Tell him to scrub it, shock it, then flush it. Then mark it in the binder." He focused on Laura again. "We try to get the riders out before the heat of the day when the scheduling works."

"I forgot how hot it gets in Texas." She was sure it wouldn't be long before she found herself wishing cowgirl attire included shorts rather than jeans.

"I was reminded the other day that Rose likes to sidestep into you when you cinch her saddle." Levi went to tighten the belly strap on the horse, and true to his word, Rose edged toward him.

Levi led the mare, now ready to ride, to a hitching post in the shade just outside the stable. "You haven't been back to Sweetheart Creek since you were a kid?"

Laura shook her head. "Not really. I flew in for the odd Thanksgiving over the years, but Luanne loved coming to New York. She found it exciting."

"Sounds like her." Levi led another horse from its stall, tossing a saddle blanket over its back. This mare was shorter than Rose, and Laura tugged the blanket straight from her side of the beast.

"How's it going with the house?" Levi asked, swinging a saddle up onto the horse's back.

"Slow." Yesterday she'd spent hours walking from room to room, opening doors and drawers and simply staring at everything. She needed a plan. One that included what to do with the diaries, old letters and photo albums she'd come across. They felt too personal to destroy or give away.

"When do you think you'll be done?" Levi asked, securing the saddle.

She had swapped the horse's halter for a bridle, and now rose up on tiptoe to say over the horse's back, "Wondering how much time you have to find a new riding manager?"

He lifted his head, his eyes crinkling. There was something about his expression that made her want to smile back.

He patted the flank of the horse. "What's this one's name?"

"Clover." She stroked the zigzag white-and-gray pattern on the animal's long nose. "I'm hoping to head home the weekend after next, if possible." She had a few things to attend to there. But she planned to return to Sweetheart Creek afterward and stay on a bit longer.

"I don't have much time then."

She shifted her weight, feeling slightly guilty. "Settling up here will likely take longer than the two weeks I've scheduled, but I figured I'd better set a goal or else I'll end up here for years."

"Would that be so bad?"

"Probably not." Her investments could keep her afloat without needing to work again if she stayed in a small town where the cost of living was low. But was that what she wanted? While she knew she'd like to settle down, she wasn't quite ready for a full and complete end to her old life.

Laura led Clover over to where Rose was hitched, fighting the urge to wince as her feet protested the new boots. She had zipped into Blue Tumbleweed when the store opened at eight-thirty, and chosen the pair of boots from the window display. She'd been assured by the owner that they would break in quickly, but was suspicious that Jenny's definition of "quickly" was a week or two off of hers, the way her feet were feeling.

"How's your nose?" she asked Levi when she returned to the barn. It still looked thicker than it should.

"Fine."

"That was a hard hit."

"How's your head?"

"Goose egg." She raised a hand to the tender bump on the back, under her ball cap. "Obviously you're hardheaded."

"So I've been told." They shared a smile that made her stomach warm, and she resisted the urge to lower her chin and bite her lip. Maintaining eye contact with Levi stirred something within her, and she was finding it required a fair amount of effort to act as though being around him didn't make her want to flirt outrageously. He was the kind of man she wanted to have hold her just so she would know how it felt, how it would change her.

Levi paused for a second, taking her in with a long, fluid gaze. Then his eyebrows flicked upward.

"What?" she said, feeling as though she'd been caught with her thoughts broadcasted across her face. Flirtatious fun was on the agenda, but she was going to have to break him in slowly, judging by how red his face had turned when she'd left her lipstick on his coffee cup earlier.

"You're…unexpected."

"How so?" She liked the idea that he might be reassessing her.

He shrugged, still studying her while slowly coiling a thick rope used for leading a horse around the ring.

"Regretting not agreeing to give me Mrs. Fisher's suggested tour of town?" she teased.

His expression grew shuttered. "No."

She felt the sting of rejection as he turned his back, and she struggled not to take it personally.

He said slowly, "But if you want one—"

"I was flirting with you, Levi. Don't get your jeans in a knot." She reached up and began fussing with some leads hanging on a hook.

"I don't think I'm quite what you're looking for," he added awkwardly. "Most of my hours are involved with the ranch, and right now I just don't have time for anything but keeping this place running."

There was that look of pressure weighing on him again. But seriously, had it been so long since a woman flirted with him that he'd forgotten it could be harmless fun?

"You don't have time to flirt?" she asked lightly.

"Are you taking this seriously?" he asked.

"What makes you think I'm not?" She knew how to saddle a horse, and so far had been scoring one hundred percent on the horse names and other details.

She caught him giving her feet a pointed look, no doubt aware of just how much the new boots were killing her.

"You prefer to wear shoes that get ruined in riding arenas," he said at long last, his expression regretful.

"I wasn't exactly expecting to jump in and save the day when I came to bring you those cookies."

Levi looked away and inhaled slowly. Laura sighed, annoyed that they couldn't seem to tap into their more playful sides, and were instead getting on each other's nerves.

"Your boots are also for show," he said quietly, as though hating to make his point.

Laura gritted her teeth. "I know." Jenny had tried to guide her toward some plain brown boots, saying they'd be kinder on her feet and last longer, but Laura had decided these prettier ones were something she could wear again back in New York.

"The riding program is important to my grandfather. He depends on this ranch and this program."

"I *know.*"

"It's hard work, and I'm relying on you to take it seriously."

They stared at each other for a long moment. "You believe that because I've been a model and like pretty boots I can't work hard and will let you down?"

He was silent for a telling beat.

She thumped her hand on a loose wall board, making the animals still in their stalls shift at the sound. If he only knew how hard being a model was. Holding awkward poses under hot lights for what felt like an eternity, while people made comments about your body, and prodded at it like it wasn't an important part of you.

"It *is* possible for a woman to be blessed with brains *and* beauty, as well as have the ability to adapt to new situations. We can be more than how we look or what we wear."

Levi's eyes blazed into hers in a way that made her adrenaline spike and her pulse race.

"I know," he said evenly.

She jammed her hands on her hips, sensing that she should shut up and walk away. "You think I'm a princess, and that you're going to have to rescue me if I take on this job. I'm just another problem on your big, long list."

His gaze dropped to her feet again, as though he was remembering those ridiculous heels she'd been wearing when they'd met.

"Maybe I was being nice by saying yes," she added. "Maybe I don't have time to fix problems for assumptive, hypocritical, stereotype-loving jerks who lack backup plans for what they keep saying is such an oh-so-important part of their ranch!" She gestured wildly, blinking back tears of rage, confused over how personal everything suddenly felt.

Levi inhaled so deeply he leaned back in his boots.

She stepped away, waving her hands in frustration. Why was she fighting with him? She didn't even *want* him to consider her as a partner or a full-time employee. But at the same time, the way she felt discounted was pushing every button she had.

"And for your information, a woman can take care of her appearance as well as flirt with a man without expecting a ring out of the deal. It's called having fun, in case you've forgotten. So check your ego at the door, buster."

A loud guffaw bounced off the wooden walls of the stable as Carmichael appeared around the corner. "I like this one." He grinned as he appraised her. "You remind me of my dear Ruth."

Mortified to have had her outburst overheard, Laura didn't know whether to stalk off into the ring and prove Levi wrong, or to flee and never return.

Levi's mouth opened, then closed, his bright blue eyes electrified.

Laura continued to glare at him, deciding that Levi and his assumptions were not going to win. She was going to show him what she was made of.

"I'll be in the ring, waiting for the riders to arrive, because despite what you assume, I do take working with special-needs children seriously."

LEVI SHUT himself in Betty's small office, fuming at Laura as well as himself.

He should go out to the arena and tell her to take a hike; he didn't need her yelling at him and taking things personally.

And how had it gotten so personal so quickly, anyway? The two of them as a couple was laughable, and if she knew that—which he thought she did—then why had she gotten her pretty lace panties tied in a bunch when he'd wanted to work, not flirt?

Man, she had a way of getting under his skin.

He was not assumptive. And he didn't have double standards, either.

He groaned, mentally kicking himself. No, he was, and he did.

He'd also fallen for the stereotype. But look at her boots! Of course he'd made assumptions, based on them along with those sexy red heels that were a danger to walk in, and had sent her flying into the ditch on Saturday. It was a wonder she hadn't been seriously hurt.

He might be all the things she'd accused him of being, but that didn't mean he needed her pointing it out. He had a lot of people depending on this ranch. Both his parents had retired, along with his granddad, expecting to pull a monthly income from the money *he* brought in. The riding program covered its own expenses for the most part, but if they lost clients because Laura didn't take it seriously that could put the program in peril. And that would break his granddad's heart.

The truth was, Levi knew he'd been raised better than to make assumptions about Laura as he had, and she had come in goodwill, to help pull him out of a tight bind.

He needed to apologize. Grovel if need be.

Had all those years of fending off Jackie Moorhouse made him fear flirting with a beautiful woman? That if he let go and had fun for a few minutes he'd somehow find himself walking down the aisle with the wrong woman before he even had the chance to catch his breath?

Shaking his head, Levi poured himself a cup of coffee from the pot near the door, but before he took a sip he set the cup back on the table, sloshing hot liquid over his hand.

Why was it that, even though he found her frustrating, he'd wanted to sweep her up and kiss her for caring enough to take him to task?

And those tears that had welled in her eyes before she'd ruthlessly blinked them back while defending herself had been like an arrow to his heart.

He needed to apologize. Now.

He picked up his cup to keep his hands occupied, so he didn't do something stupid like kiss her or touch her soft hair when he went out there.

But before he could leave Betty's office, his youngest brother, a teacher at Sweetheart Creek High School, entered the office.

"Don't you have classes to teach?" Levi asked, checking his watch. He knew Ryan got some bonus release time to compensate for the hours he spent coaching the football team after school, but he rarely came by the ranch during the day.

"Good to see you, too. Who's the hottie in the fancy new boots? Is that Laura Oakes?"

He nodded.

"She bent over to grab a bridle, and Granddad nearly had a coronary." Ryan flopped into Betty's computer chair and swung his booted feet onto her desk. "She your new Betty?"

"For the time being." He knocked his brother's boots off the desk with more gusto than was required. "She's not staying."

"Because of you?"

Levi scowled. "She's from New York City, and she's completely impractical in every way." He was getting irritated again, thinking about those blue boots and how striking she looked with a flush of anger brightening her cheeks.

Ryan narrowed his eyes, a sure sign he was shifting out of get-under-his-older-brother's-skin mode and into thinking mode. "How so?"

"Her shoes."

"She was wearing boots."

He needed to have a word with Jenny Oliver about the way she'd seen city gal Laura coming and hadn't pointed her toward real working boots.

"Laura's a princess," Levi stated.

"Granddad said she ran into the ring the other day and settled Bronwyn and Cherry after giving you a bloody nose." Ryan's grin made Levi want to make use of his knuckles. "I think I like city princesses. I may have to find one for myself. Is she available?"

Levi closed his eyes, striving for inner calm. "Don't you have some hormonal teens to teach? I have problems to solve."

"Right." Ryan stood, suddenly serious. "I came to tell you the windmill's broken."

"Which one? Windmill six is being serviced today." The mills pumped water into troughs for the herds. This time of year one could be down for a day or two and the cattle would be fine, as there were alternate water sources in the pastures they were in for fall feeding. But in the middle of a heat wave or after a storm that made the trails impassable, not having a windmill pumping water could quickly become a dire situation.

"The one up by Devil's Horn."

They would have to move the herd that was up there if the mill didn't get fixed in the next several days. Levi made a mental note to ask Hank to round them up and move them into the pasture closest to the ranch.

"When were you up there?" he asked Ryan.

"No reason."

"I asked when, not why." His brother liked to use the overlook as a private date area, and Levi bet he had taken a woman up for a little kiss-and-tell, as Myles referred to it.

"Thought you'd want to know it's not turning in the wind."

"You gonna fix it?" Ryan was the family mastermind when it came to tinkering with stuff like windmills. Levi could figure it out, but his brother could break his fix-it record every time. And, technically, he owned just as big of a slice of the ranch and its problems as Levi did.

Ryan glanced at his watch. "I have a class to teach. See ya."

"Is that a no?"

Ryan shrugged. He liked the ranch, but it was obvious his heart wasn't into its daily operations. Sometimes Levi wished he could just walk away, like his brothers did. Pop by whenever he wanted. Then again, if he wasn't on the ranch, what else would he do? Where would he go? Ranching was his life, his identity, his joy—even when it caused him stress headaches.

"Maybe I should hire someone to take care of regular maintenance items like the fences and windmills. We can't afford to lose cattle, and Myles, Hank and myself aren't keeping up with things very well."

"Get Granddad to help. He knows this stuff. He built half of it."

"He's seventy-nine."

"He's not dead yet."

Levi nodded, knowing he couldn't convince Ryan in just one conversation that their aging grandfather simply wasn't able to contribute in the ways he had even a few years ago.

"Game Friday?" he asked.

"Yup."

"Gonna win?"

"Always." Ryan grinned, his confidence nestled solidly in the team's envious win-loss ratio. He set up the strategy for the plays, while their brother Myles worked as the paid assistant coach, coming in to run drills. During the season, the principal cut Ryan's hours in the classroom so he could focus on football, giving him a bonus as well. To say the sport was big in town was an understatement. So there was a lot riding on their performance, as well as the team's. Personally, Levi would rather have the pressures of the ranch.

"You coming?" Ryan asked. "Jackie's been asking after you."

"She's been asking after any Wylder with a Y chromosome under the age of forty."

Ryan smirked. "I think she's holding out for Cole's return."

Levi turned and added more coffee to his cup, filling it almost to the brim. "I'll be there. Sitting at center field. Assuming nothing else breaks around here. Speaking of which, we need to talk about the future of this place. I can't keep running it on my own forever."

"Yeah, sure." His brother was already out the door. A half beat later, he leaned back in. "Oh, and don't upset the princess. I saw her with Donnie." His look told Levi he was giving her a mighty big thumbs-up about how she was managing their most difficult client.

"She's out there with Donnie?" The kid was twice her weight and got aggressive when faced with change. He hadn't been able to stay in school due to his behavior issues despite Ryan's attempts to help.

"Don't go interfering and thinking you know best. She's doing great," Ryan called.

But Levi was already on his way, his heart thundering. He had forgotten about Donnie, and he feared what he might see when he arrived ringside.

The late morning sunshine hit him hard when he stepped outdoors, and it took a moment for his eyes to adjust, giving him long enough to calm himself a fraction before spotting Laura.

She *was* doing great. Donnie was chatting to her a mile a minute, trying to impress the new grown-up in his life. He looked as at home on the horse as if he'd grown up riding. Laura was listening as she led him around the ring, like they'd done it all a thousand times.

Levi shook his head in wonder. There was something about this beautiful city gal that was going to make him have to rethink everything.

LAURA WAS HELPING Donnie dismount when Levi appeared at the riding ring's fence. His face was a lot less stormy than it had been earlier, yet just as handsome with this new, unreadable expression.

He shifted his hat higher when she gave him a questioning look, before turning her back to him to keep an eye on the other riders.

Moments later, out of the corner of her eye, she saw Levi angle toward the gate that allowed access into the riding arena. Something was up, but she didn't think it had to do with Donnie, who was now standing beside her, helmet still on, chin strap nestled against his lower jaw. He'd done amazingly well, as far as she could tell, and on the other side of the railing his grandmother was watching, smiling with tears in her eyes, hands clenched together at her chest.

"How's it going, Donnie?" Levi asked as he drew near.

The youth grinned and gave two thumbs-up before awkwardly running across the uneven turf in his cowboy boots, leading the horse away.

Laura moved to intervene, unsure if it was okay for him to run with the animal. A cowboy she hadn't met yet, and who looked like a bulkier version of Levi, appeared in the doorway of the stable, giving her a nod. She dropped back, wishing she could help Donnie rather than stay and face Levi. She turned to him, arms crossed.

"What's up?"

"Things go okay with Donnie?" Levi asked.

"Yes." She held his eyes, daring him to find fault.

He was holding a cup of coffee, and as he forgot about it the liquid spilled over the rim, splashing his boots. He righted the cup, head tipped toward the stables. "That's my brother Myles," he said, gesturing to the man helping Donnie take Clover inside.

"He seems familiar. Did he hang out at the swimming hole as a teen?"

Levi nodded. "Yeah, he used to sneak out of chores on the hot days. Although that was mostly Ryan. He's the youngest and likes to make his own rules."

Was Myles here to take over her position? Because oddly

enough, she'd enjoyed being out here with the kids, her mind blessedly blank, her smile at the ready to share in their joy. Despite having to see Levi again, she was hoping to come back tomorrow.

"How many brothers do you have?" she asked.

"Four."

"Wow. Five boys. And you're the bossy, responsible eldest, I'm guessing?"

He nodded, his mouth tightening. "Do you have siblings?" he asked.

She stared at him for a moment. "A sister. Same age—stepsister, actually, but she's like blood to me."

He nodded again, then shifted his hat like he had earlier. "I don't do this very often."

"Do what?"

"Apologize."

"And are you going to try it now?" Her arms were still crossed and she stuck out her right hip.

"Yes."

She waited.

"I'm sorry for the way I judged you. I can already see that you're good for this riding stable, and for the riders."

She narrowed her eyes.

"I know you're leaving in a few weeks, but based on what I've seen so far, if you decide to stay longer you have a job here until Betty comes back."

A spike of pride made her want to smile, but Laura held it back, waiting to see if there was more to his apology. Realizing that was all she was going to get, she said, "Thank you."

Levi's left shoulder dropped slightly and he sighed. "And I don't truly believe you're a princess." He grumbled that last word.

"Not even a little bit?"

His eyes tracked to her dust-covered boots. Finally he looked up. "Honestly, I'm not sure. I want to say yes, but I'm afraid to."

He gave her a half smile and any anger she still had toward him slid away.

She shifted her aching feet. "Well, I am a princess. A little bit. Sometimes. But not always." She shook her head at her awkwardness. Suddenly she felt bashful, as if letting down their barriers for a moment had somehow made her old crush feel extra large and omnipresent again.

She looked away when Levi squinted at her as though trying to decide whether she was trying to trap him with her admission.

"You have seen my boots?" she asked, her cheeks flushing.

"I need to talk to Jenny about that. It's not right to take advantage of someone from out of town who doesn't know any better."

"No, she did fine." Laura placed a hand on his forearm. His indignation on her behalf was endearing.

"This was all me, not Jenny. My inner princess made a valid point that won over my more practical side. I thought I'd be able to wear these again in the city." She twisted her leg to show off the white stitching that created a floral pattern up the side of the aquamarine leather. It wasn't so white any longer. "You can take a girl out of the city, but you can't make her a cowgirl overnight." Laura laughed, not caring how Levi judged her for her boots, or anything else. Life was too darn short, and honestly, she'd proved herself in the ring, as well as in other areas of her life. She didn't need his approval.

A ghost of a smile haunted his lips. "Can I get you a sweet tea?" he asked.

She waited a beat, considering the olive branch. She nodded. "I'd like that. Thanks."

Laura gazed around the ring, realizing she still had horses and riders to take care of. Donnie and Clover had gone in, but the other two riders had taken advantage of her distraction and were still circling the arena, despite prompts from their ringside parents telling them it was time to go. "Let me finish up here."

"Myles can do it." Levi seemed to catch himself. "He'll help show you what to do. And once you're free, come meet me at the house."

He paused for a moment, then with a tip of his hat, headed off. If she was into betting, she'd wager she'd gotten under his skin, and he wasn't sure what to do about having a city gal hone in on territory he'd reserved for a verified, Texas-born, ranch-loving cowgirl.

5

<hr>

*L*evi watched Laura work for a short while, then went to the house to get a snack before she came in for sweet tea. He wasn't sure why he'd suggested it, other than he supposed he was trying to make amends—a task he seemed in need of doing each time he spent any time with her.

He bit into a crisp apple, licking away the juice that dribbled over his lip, then rubbed his belly. It did seem a bit more hollow than it used to. Maybe Laura's kitchen skills stretched further than just baking and she might have time to cook for the ranch, as well. He was getting tired of his brothers nixing his ideas to hire out more jobs around the ranch, their fear of overextending the budget very real. However, Levi felt if they wanted to reach the ranch's true potential they were going to need to replace the people who'd left, at the very least. And that included his mother, the cook.

If Laura could cook, that might keep her close to the ranch, too.

Keep her close to the ranch?

Just because she had accepted his awful apology didn't mean she was ready to jump into his arms. Or that he wanted her to.

She was just solving problems for him around the ranch, which made her a very welcome guest.

Either way, he hoped it took Laura a fair bit of time to sell her aunt's house. And not just so he wouldn't have to find her replacement.

Myles ambled in, scratching his midriff. "Anything to eat?"

"I thought you were helping Laura?"

"She's fine." He pulled open the fridge door, bending and staring into the cold cavern as though hoping some of their mother's lasagna would magically appear. Levi had done the same thing yesterday.

Myles straightened, arching his back. "We should get a fridge with the freezer on the bottom."

"I was thinking we should hire a cook."

"I like that idea."

"Yeah?"

"Yeah. We'd save money because we wouldn't be eating out all the time."

That seemed like sound logic. Maybe the four brothers could go in on a cook together, since the off-ranch ones, Ryan and Brant, ended up eating out more now as well. Even though Brant lived above his veterinary clinic in town, he had often come by the ranch for supper, as their mom had always laid out feasts, welcoming anyone with Wylder blood to pop by for the evening meal. Maybe she was cooking big spreads at her place in town and none of them had clued in yet.

"Hey," Levi said, "what was that weird text I got from you about a roll of wire in the towel rack?"

Myles frowned at him in confusion. "What?"

"The text you sent this morning. You need to talk slower into your phone so it dictates your words more accurately."

"Oh! Right. I took care of the fence down by the creek. I added another roll of wire to the tab over at the store."

That made more sense.

"How are we for fence posts?"

"Good." He had found a can of soda and popped the tab, downing half of it while leaning against the kitchen counter. Looking refreshed, he smiled and checked the time on the cow-shaped clock on the wall. "Well, gotta run. Football practice starts in a few hours and I've gotta see if the shop teacher will let me use his equipment to fix a broken weld on the coaching command tower."

"Can you grab Grandma's old saddle blanket from the barn?" Levi asked. "Josie said she could stitch up that corner Clover chewed if we drop it off at her tack shop."

His brother nodded.

"Thanks."

The screen door banged shut as he left, then opened again, its hinge's once ear-piercing squeak now gone thanks to a little attention from Levi and an oil can.

"Forget to ask me for a lunch order?" he called to Myles. "I'll take whatever Mrs. Fisher has on special." Today was Monday. That meant double burger with cheese. His stomach growled in anticipation.

"Myles is bringing lunch?" Brant asked, appearing around the corner. "The brat didn't take my order." He eyed the kitchen and then the empty fruit bowl. "I was hoping you'd gone shopping."

Slightly shorter than Levi, with the same dark brown hair, Brant began digging through the fridge, pulling out a stack of sandwich meat, some hot dogs and what looked like fresh steak. He shoved it all back in. "Ever heard of scurvy?"

"Is that what happens to brothers who complain about the food in someone else's house?"

Brant raised his brows, uncapping a bottle of beer. "What happened to your speech about us all owning this place and needing to figure it out?"

"We do. But you can start complaining about the fridge

contents when you start adding to them, or give me the okay on hiring a cook."

"You go find Cole and we'll get the ranch sorted out." Brant had tried to convince the second-eldest Wylder to return from his several-year hiatus when their dad had remarried a few months ago. Without saying as much, they'd all waited for Cole to show up in South Carolina for the ceremony, but he hadn't. In fact, as far as Levi knew, nobody had even heard from him since Brant had tracked him down in some mountain town out west called Blueberry Springs.

"We might not be able to wait for him forever, you know." Levi shoved his hat farther back on his head and fought the anger and frustration he felt. Cole had been like a twin to him, and they'd made a great team. Despite not seeing his brother for years, there were times Levi would find himself looking up, expecting to find Cole at his side while working on a fence line or breaking in a new horse. Other times he'd catch himself reaching for his phone to text Cole, wanting to run a scenario past him, as he always brought a different perspective to Levi's problems. But Cole had left after they'd had a fight—uncharacteristic for both of them—and hadn't been back since.

"And you know he won't come home if I ask," he added gruffly.

"I think the opposite." Brant took a sip of the beer and made a face, then looked at the label.

"Yeah, well. You don't know everything."

"I know plenty."

"Do you?" They locked gazes for a beat before Levi looked away.

"What is this crap?" Brant held out the bottle.

"Ryan's Lambic beer."

"Is that the stuff where he leaves the wort uncovered overnight so airborne yeast gets in it for fermentation?"

"Yup."

"Serves me right for having a beer before noon." He poured the drink down the drain. "And doesn't he know what kind of yeasts and bacteria are in the air around ranches? Gross, man."

Levi shrugged. "So the woman in the stables is helping out for a while."

"You mean Laura?"

"Yeah. She heads back to NYC in about two weeks unless her aunt's house takes longer to sort out. So if you know of a riding program manager I could use—*we* could use one."

"So crazy-hair-Laura grew up, huh?" Brant gestured to his own hat-covered head as though miming big hair.

"Her hair's nice."

"Remember that summer when she was underfoot in the hardware store with all of those questions? You called her Little Miss Build It or something."

"Little Miss Project."

"That was it."

Levi had admired Laura's go-get-it-done attitude, and how she was helping her elderly, but spry, aunt. She'd had traits he'd found himself seeking in others. Maybe that's where his assumptions had gone off track earlier. He'd forgotten about teenaged Laura and had gotten caught up in grown-up Laura's fake nails and highlights. People didn't change, did they? On the inside she was still that get-it-done persona who was about lots more than her glamorous appearance, wasn't she?

That idea lifted his heart in a way he figured would likely get him in trouble. She admitted she still had some princess traits, and she'd soon be leaving town. In his world those were two warning bells.

"She had a major crush on you," Brant said.

"She what?" Levi perked up. No. Not Laura. "She's going back home soon. To New York. And I'm busy. Busy keeping this ranch from falling in on itself."

Brant stared at him, as if expecting Levi to admit to something.

"She's selling Luanne's place," Levi said firmly, "and going *home*."

"Really?" Brant's tone held a note of I-know-something-you-might-not.

"Really. That's why she's here. To get the place on the market. Sell it and get out, like, yesterday."

"She's not in a hurry," Brant said. He was wiping down the sticky counter. "This is disgusting. Do you know how quickly germs multiply in conditions like this?"

Levi stole the cloth from his brother. Brant was on a real germ kick today, which likely meant he'd gone on a farm call and found something disgusting that Levi didn't want to hear about. "How do you know she's not in a hurry?"

Brant paused, as though deciding whether to share what he knew with Levi. "She turned down an offer on the house."

"It's already listed for sale?"

He shook his head.

"Then how do you know an offer was made and rejected?"

"Because I made it."

"What?" Levi felt gutted with betrayal. "I need her here. Why would you do that?"

Brant smiled. "Maybe she wants to spend a little time in Sweetheart Creek getting her boots dirty, after all."

"Was your offer a test?" That was a pretty pricey one, if so.

Brant's expression hinted that he'd actually wanted the house. But why? He had a perfectly good place above the clinic all five brothers had helped him build.

"Think she's single?" Brant asked.

Levi narrowed his eyes.

His brother's smile had grown even larger. It faded slightly as he peered at Levi. "Hey, what happened to your nose?"

Levi cupped a hand over the bruised skin. "She's not your type." His words came out forced and firm.

"Don't worry about it," Brant said, heading for the door. "I can tell you've already called dibs."

"I have *not* called dibs," Levi muttered to the empty room. Seriously? He had not called dibs on the intriguing and beautiful Laura Oakes, and he never would. They were like fire and water. Like a rainstorm and a dust storm.

He stomped across the room in frustration, throwing Brant's cloth into the sink. Why had his parents had so many boys, anyway? Why hadn't they stopped having kids after being blessed with him?

The front door opened again, and Levi held his tongue in case it was Laura.

"Maybe she doesn't have a date for the barn dance," Brant called. "Give your going-to-town duds a little dusting off and take her for a spin across the dance floor."

"You know I don't do long-distance relationships." Tried that. Failed miserably. For two long years he'd waited for Janet after she'd left for college in California, believing she'd return when she graduated with her biology degree. She'd said it was backup in case her future career in ranching went belly-up. Turned out it was a backup for her acting career, and she was busy changing her last name to Keys, falling in love with Hollywood, glitz and glamor and another actor. She didn't return, and in hindsight Levi felt he'd been naive to think his love would be enough to bring her home again.

And he liked to believe he was smart enough not to repeat his past mistakes.

HAVING BRUSHED down Clover and the other horses, Laura set them out to graze, then sat on a pile of bales stacked along the wall opposite the horse stalls, wishing she hadn't checked her phone.

She closed her eyes and inhaled slowly, trying to retain some poise, which the tabloids had tried to strip from her. With trembling fingers, she brushed a tendril of hair behind her ear. She knew the article one of her old friends had texted her wasn't true, and that the rumors would blow over even if they managed to take hold. It was just the tabloids looking to sell papers. She had not experienced a breakdown, and she was not homeless, either.

Well, she was. But she wasn't.

The photo they'd dug up, of her sitting beside a homeless man in an alley, was out of context. It had been taken during an awareness campaign a few years ago, when she and several other celebrities had camped out on the streets of New York for one long, cold November night to bring attention to the closing of some homeless shelters.

The quote from her ex-boyfriend, though? That stung. And yes, sometimes even she would say whatever came to mind to get a reporter off her back. Like the one that had hounded her when she'd been moving out of her apartment last week. When he'd asked if she planned to have kids now that she was retired, she'd turned her fear that she'd never find the right man to start a family with into an off-hand joke. It was too late for her, she'd told him, but who wanted kids when you were off to travel the world and live a glamorous jet-set life, anyway?

Meanwhile Memphis had all but said she was living in her car after breaking up with him and moving out in a fit.

Yeah, a fit because he'd betrayed her trust by lining up his next girlfriend while still living with Laura. She couldn't believe he'd stooped to giving the tabloid a quote—assuming they hadn't tricked him into it.

Laura let out a shaky breath and stood up. She was here in Texas, and all that tabloid mess was…elsewhere. Being a celebrity always welcomed the negative, and her motto had always been to match it with something positive.

So find the positive.

Helping out here was one. And maybe Levi would allow her to volunteer her time instead of paying her, so she'd be more than a stopgap to his current absent-manager issue. That would be another positive.

"Excuse me? Miss Laura?"

Donnie's grandmother, Wilma, came into the stable and Laura dusted herself off, placing a smile where her frown had been. She was sure she'd seen the woman leave with Donnie at least half an hour ago.

"Yes, what can I do for you? Did your car break down?"

"Not today," she said with a weary smile. "I meant to talk to Betty last week about Donnie's tuition."

"Oh, um..." Levi hadn't discussed any of the office tasks with her.

"I didn't want to mention this in front of Donnie, as he might get upset, and I should probably talk to Levi, but it's easier to say it to you." She inhaled slowly, then said firmly and steadily, "I can't afford to bring Donnie anymore. He loves this program, and it's been great for him. So don't think it's you or the horses. It's not. Coming here is the best thing in his life. I just can't afford it any longer."

The woman sucked in her cheeks as she faced Laura.

"Did Betty tell you about the scholarship program?" Laura asked.

"Scholarship?" Her eyes widened slightly.

"It's new." Laura thought quickly, creating one on the spot. "It covers outreach programs for children who..." She shrugged, unable to come up with the right word. "Anyway, Donnie might be eligible. We can apply on your behalf if you'd like."

"Would you do that?"

"Certainly." Laura nodded briskly. There it was. Something

positive to combat the negative. "Just keep bringing Donnie while we deal with the application process."

"What if he doesn't get a scholarship?"

"Then we won't worry about the tuition for the rides while we're waiting to hear back. We'll cover it."

"I couldn't put you out by not paying." Wilma's eyes had filled with concern. "I pay my bills. I don't take handouts."

"I understand. I'm sure Donnie is a shoe-in, and since this is a new scholarship I doubt there's much competition yet." She gave her a reassuring smile. Laura didn't know what the riding program tuition came to, but was certain she could cover it. Seeing the way Donnie changed while riding Clover was worth more than any dollar amount.

Laura walked his grandmother to her car, chatting about Texas and the heat, then headed back through the stable. As she went, she inhaled the unique aromas of animals, hay and sunbaked wood. She paused to brush her hand down the mane of a large appaloosa named Poppy that was stable-bound until a ligament had a chance to heal. From what she'd heard from Myles and Hank, the ranch's hired hand, kittens had gotten underfoot over the weekend and the horse had gone down when one tried to climb its leg.

Laura inhaled one last time, promising herself she wouldn't give the tabloids another thought, and headed out of the stable. She followed a worn path that wound through a grove of tall oak trees, taking her to the back of the older ranch-style home. It had a stately, rambling feel, partially due to its various additions, the most recent appearing to be a large stone patio that spread out from the back door, running almost fifty feet along the length of the house. There was a grill, a seating area with outdoor couches shaded by a large canopy, and planted vines. It looked like a perfect spot for a social gathering, and she wondered how often Levi entertained. From what she'd deduced it was just Levi, his brother Myles and their grandfather living here, with the ranch hand, Hank, residing in one of the staff cabins on the next quarter section.

Laura followed a stone walkway around to the front of the house and took the three steps up to the door. She knocked twice, then walked in, as was the custom in these parts. It felt intrusive, yet somehow as though she was part of an exclusive club, not only expected, but welcome.

The cool air inside was a welcome relief. "Hello?" she called, taking in the large entry, which overlooked an open, sunken living room and several hallways that branched off into various wings. The floor was tiled in a dark brown, the living room decorated in earthy tones and furnished to easily seat sixteen around a tall stone fireplace.

"Hey," Levi said, coming around a corner from her left. "How did it go?"

"Pretty good I think." She ran her hands down the thighs of her jeans, feeling oddly nervous. Suddenly what he thought of her ability in the arena seemed important.

"Follow me," he said, leading her in the direction he'd come from, into a large kitchen with white cupboards, a sizable island with a sink and more cupboards and counter space than you'd ever find in most New York kitchens. Everything was definitely bigger in Texas.

She moved to the large dining table laid out along a bank of windows that overlooked the patio she'd been admiring earlier. She took one of the ten chairs and sat.

Levi went to the fridge and got out a glass pitcher filled with sweet tea, waving it in her direction. She nodded, picking at her chipped nail polish. As he had predicted, her manicure hadn't lasted long once she'd started working in the stables.

"I offered to pay Donnie's tuition," she said, deciding it was best to let him know immediately. "His grandma said she couldn't afford to keep bringing him, and it's clear how much this program means to them both."

"How did Wilma respond to that?" he asked, glancing over his shoulder for a moment.

"I lied."

Levi crossed the kitchen, his boots clacking on the tile floor. He set a stein filled with tea in front of her. "You lied?"

She shrugged. "Seemed like she'd be too proud to take a handout. So I created a scholarship on the spot. Anyway, it's taken care of. Just let me know how much to transfer into the program's account as payment. Then I'll let Wilma know Donnie got the scholarship."

Levi simply stared at her. Finally, he said, "That was mighty generous of you."

"Donnie needs it." She tucked a strand of hair behind her ear, then, realizing she was still wearing her ball cap, took it off. "If you feel it would benefit others, I could create a real scholarship."

"You're doing plenty already, and you won't be earning a dime at this rate."

"You don't need to pay me."

"I do."

"It's fun."

"It's not a volunteer position."

Laura took a sip of her sweet tea.

"I was serious about what I said earlier," Levi stated. "As long as you want to stay, you're most welcome. But don't go changing things. Betty won't appreciate it. And I recommend you keep the scholarship on the hush-hush."

"Why?"

"People won't take kindly to a newcomer…" He paused, licked his lips, then said gently, "Your generosity could be taken the wrong way. I know you just want to help, and that is very much appreciated. But keep in mind that we Texans pride ourselves on being able to take care of our own, if you know what I mean."

She did. Nobody liked a newcomer popping up and throwing around money and making everyone feel incompetent or poor.

"I promise my scholarship won't cause problems."

He watched her for another long moment, then gave a nod. "Thank you for doing that for Donnie." His expression softened and she could see she'd won some points with him, even though the scholarship caused Levi some concerns. "I have a proposal," he added.

Laura placed a hand against her chest as though surprised. "But we've only just met!"

It took Levi a second to catch her joke about a marriage proposal, and he rewarded her with a half smile. Okay, so he wasn't a big joker when he was being Mr. Serious. Which was pretty much most of the time by the look of things.

"Do you cook?" he asked.

"Sort of. Why?"

"We need one."

"For an event?" She involuntarily glanced toward the stone patio on her left. She'd always wanted to entertain back in New York, but her apartment had been too small, and to rent a place was pricey. This house would lend itself well for entertaining, but a caterer she most definitely was not.

"Someone for me, Myles, Carmichael and our current ranch hand, Hank. Lunch and supper. Sometimes my other brothers pop in, or we have extra staff for whatever's going on seasonally. Everyone's getting tired of my steaks. Apparently they're afraid of scurvy."

Laura cracked a smile, and Levi did as well.

She caught herself looking out at the patio again. "What happened to your last chef?"

"My mom used to do the cooking, but she's living in town now."

"And she doesn't cook anymore?"

Levi opened his mouth, tipped his head to the side, then closed it again. From the quirking of his lips she could pick up a hint of remorse. From what she'd gathered, this ranch had once been a thriving, bustling place full of life and love.

Levi was a proud man, and that may have prevented him from doing the obvious.

Doubting herself, as she'd likely overstepped more than enough times for the day, she pulled in a deep breath and risked putting her poor, tender foot in her mouth with her idea. "Instead of hiring someone, have you considered asking your mom to come back home?"

LEVI THOUGHT about Laura's suggestion. But why would his mother want to return to the ranch? She knew she was welcome; this place was as much Maria's as anyone's. She had earned her retirement, settled into a new home and a routine that was far less grueling than the nonstop work of a ranch. The last thing she probably needed was to start cooking for the boys again.

"She's retired," he explained to Laura. "It's a nice thought, though."

"There's no harm in asking. Is there?"

"I suppose not," he admitted, appreciating her sincerity and willingness to help him solve his problem when she likely had plenty of her own to deal with.

Had he noticed earlier how much he liked this woman?

"You ask her, and in the meantime if I hear of anyone I'll let you know."

"I'd appreciate it." Levi went to the kitchen island and poured himself a glass of sweet tea. "I heard you got an offer on Luanne's place."

Laura shifted in her chair, fingering the condensation on the outside of her glass.

"It wasn't good?" He still had no clue why his brother would want to buy the place. It felt odd, but so did her refusal. She was staying only a few weeks, wasn't she?

Laura opened her mouth, her eyes searching the wall across from her as though trying to sort out what to say. Finally, she just shrugged.

Levi sat, then leaned forward, waiting for her to speak, before realizing he was inhaling her sweet smell. She was part hair products and part outdoors, no perfume today. It was a nice mix.

"The offer didn't feel right. You know how vultures sweep in as soon as something is hinted at going up for sale, and try a lowball amount to see if you're desperate? It felt like that."

Brant definitely wasn't a vulture.

"So you haven't listed it yet?" he confirmed.

"I'm not ready." Laura's gaze dropped to her hands. "As weird as it sounds, making sure I find someone who cares about Luanne's house is the least I can do in return for all she's done for me over the years."

"That makes sense to me. Did you find out anything about the potential buyer?"

"It was a young family, which made saying no difficult."

A young family? Levi really needed to have a chat with his single brother.

"Well, I guess you're not homeless then," he said with a smile.

Laura's face clouded over, and he wondered why. She lifted the glass to her lips and downed three quarters of the ice-cold liquid, then stood, taking the last of her drink to the sink. "This was nice. Thank you."

"I'm sorry," he said, standing in turn. "Did I say something?"

"No, no. It's fine." She was a horrible liar.

Levi rocked back on his heels, a pang echoing in his chest.

She gave a tight smile and nod of goodbye as she exited the kitchen, retracing her steps to the front door.

"Hey," Levi called, hurrying to catch up with her. She was

already across the porch and down the steps by the time he reached the closing screen door. "You okay?"

Laura turned at the car. She opened her hands at her sides, then closed them again as though wrestling with something. Finally she said, "Just feeling at odds with the world right now."

"How so?"

"You've read the article. It's not true. At least not completely."

"What article?"

"In the tabloids."

He started to laugh at the idea of him reading tabloids, then caught her expression, his amusement dying. "No. Actually, I haven't. Why?"

She shook her head and waved a hand. "Never mind. I'm just being…" She shook her head again and opened her car door.

"So they're making up stuff?" He came closer, afraid to let her go, wanting to fix whatever it was that was hurting her. "Anything interesting?"

To his surprise, she laughed. "Not really. Just taking things out of context, which seems to be their specialty."

He nodded.

"Instead of kicking out my boyfriend, which I was within my rights to do, I moved out. So now I'm without a place. Everything's either here or in storage, but he made it sound like I *could be* homeless, and then they got their hands on a photo that makes it look like I am."

"So, what you're saying is that you went out one morning, but forgot to wash your face and brush your hair?" He couldn't imagine Laura looking as though she was without a place to wash up each day. Even after a few hours in the riding arena and the heat she looked taken care of. As gorgeous as ever. Maybe even more so.

"Right now everything's just…" She shrugged and adjusted her ball cap, looking like that uncertain preteen he'd helped so many times all those summers ago. He waited for her chin to rise in defiance, but it didn't. "I was hoping I'd have some time here to sort myself out. Maybe stay…" She gave a light snort, as though dismissing an idea that might get her laughed at.

"Stay in Sweetheart Creek?" His heart surged, but her eyes fluttered closed, her long dark lashes creating shadows on her pale cheeks.

She opened her eyes again. "The town and Luanne made me feel like I belonged, and that helped me find a new direction when I was thirteen. You know, gave me hope and some big ideas about my future. I guess I was wishing for lightning to strike twice," she added quickly, a touch of vulnerability in her voice. "It's silly, I know."

Without thinking, Levi closed the distance between them and folded her in his arms, snugging her body against his as though his embrace could make her world a better place once again.

6

---

*L*aura had spent the past five days working at the Sweet Meadows Ranch in the mornings, then reading through emails and proposals from her agent at Luanne's before eating a portion of one of the casseroles that had been given to her on her arrival, then sifting through her aunt's belongings for the rest of the afternoon. More often than not, she found a reason to head down to the diner to chat with whomever happened by. Kind of like today.

"How's the house coming along?" Mrs. Fisher asked, pausing to chat during her move down the counter filling customers' coffee cups, hers included. Usually Laura had the back counter to herself, but today every stool was occupied.

"It's slow. Unlike in here. What's going on?"

"Auction day. Cattle, horses…if it has four legs it's for sale," the waitress explained. "And dealing with a loved one's estate isn't something that can be rushed, honey." She tipped her head sympathetically. Her mountain of teased hair didn't move, and Laura had a feeling the woman kept the local drugstore in healthy profits with her daily hair spray consumption.

Laura gently swirled her coffee, contemplating the dark fluid.

There was something about the diner that made her enjoy drinking it black. The bitter honesty of untouched java made her feel grounded. Or maybe it just balanced out the sweet pecan pie she had a habit of pairing with it.

She finished the last bite of her pie and slid the plate away. She had planned to leave for the city in a week, but wasn't even halfway through her great-aunt's things. And she wasn't any closer to figuring out where she wanted to settle down next. Manhattan again? Greenwich Village? Or listen to that tempting voice in her head that suggested she stay here for six months, maybe a year, maybe even longer?

At least her agent was keeping her busy with ideas for her career, so she didn't drive herself nuts with complete indecision.

Her stepsister, Ava, had offered her a spot on her couch in NYC if she ended up needing it, and having a backup plan was nice. Everyone needed a sister like hers, and hugs like Levi's. Both had given Laura the strength to carry on through her week while the tabloids had a heyday with her name and old photos.

Her phone buzzed with a message from Ava. There was a link to an article with the note: *Thought you'd want to read this one before you heard about it elsewhere.*

Would it not end? Laura took a fortifying sip of her coffee and opened the link. It went to the social column in New York's biggest newspaper. She didn't have to get far into the weekly roundup to discover she was apparently hiding out in Texas with a sizable inheritance, and had flown into a rage and dumped her boyfriend of two years for no reason.

Laura set her phone on the counter, facedown. She breathed in, then out, trying to block out the lies. Would she have to worry about the paparazzi showing up to take photos of the so-called crazed model breaking down? Maybe she was far enough into the middle of nowhere that they wouldn't venture this far and she could hide until things blew over.

Or maybe she could give some talk show host the insider

exclusive on her breakup with Memphis. Somehow she found she didn't want to play that game. Not even when she thought about how Memphis had been awful about her retirement. Or how he had often become downright pouty about her time away from him whenever she focused on her career, or how he had become insecure about her income eclipsing his. Not to mention how he had spent more and more time with her now former friend, a younger model.

Laura just wanted to hide. Start over. Find a nest of trustworthy, honest people who liked her and accepted her as she was. Whether she was rich or poor, pretty or ugly.

Two men who had been sitting beside her discussing geldings paid their tab and left. Moments later a woman Laura had met on her first day back, almost a week ago, took the vacated spot beside her.

Jackie. That was her name, and she had a thing for Levi.

If the woman had ever experienced one of his glorious hugs, no wonder she was chasing after him like an imprinted duckling. Laura had dearly needed a hug, and the way Levi had folded her into his arms had been divine. The problem was, she'd spent the following days fighting the temptation to fake a crisis so she could score another one of those wonderful embraces. The way he'd held her had made her feel as though somebody finally understood.

It was a good thing he wasn't looking for a girlfriend.

"Hello, Laura." Jackie smiled and reached over the counter to grab a clean white cup to wave at Mrs. Fisher. She was wearing a denim skirt and a red checked blouse tied at the waist, Laura noted, smiling back when the woman settled her gaze on her footwear and stated, "I love your boots."

Laura glanced down at the fashion statement. They were looking a little rough after their time in the ring all week, but they no longer hurt her feet in quite the same way. Her followers on Instagram had loved them, as well as today's update on how they were breaking in. She had the nicest people following her.

"Thank you. I got them at Blue Tumbleweed."

"I know. I've been eyeing them for weeks. They're cute."

"They are. They also pretty much killed my ability to walk for the first day and a half."

Jackie laughed. "I don't know why they can't make cowboy boots that feel great from the get-go."

"They do," Mrs. Fisher said, pausing to fill Jackie's cup before topping up Laura's again. "You two just don't like the way they look."

They all laughed.

"You going to the game tonight?" Jackie asked Laura.

"Football?" she guessed, based on the signs she'd seen around town.

"There's nothing else," Jackie confirmed.

Laura considered going. Back home she'd blend in with the crowd if she went to a Yankees game alone, but around here she was pretty sure she'd be obvious.

"I think I'll stay in," she said.

"Come with me," Jackie urged, taking her arm. "We can eat greasy food from the concession and bat our eyelashes at the eligible men."

"I just broke up with someone."

"We're just batting our lashes, not taking any of them home." Jackie lowered her voice. "Unless one of those sexy Wylder boys makes me an offer." She leaned back on her stool, exhaling a dramatic, self-pitying sigh. "I don't know what it's going to take to snare one of them."

"Try narrowing it down," Mrs. Fisher said in a dry tone as she wiped the counter. "Lift your cup, honey." She wiped the spot in front of Jackie. "You aren't going to make a man feel special if you're chasing his four brothers as well."

"Is Cole back?" Jackie asked, perking up.

"Best to move on," Mrs. Fisher said gently.

"Who's Cole?" Laura asked, once the waitress was out of hearing.

"Totally wounded brooding cowboy," Jackie replied immediately, her expression distant. But then she faked a swoon, just about falling off her stool, causing Laura to giggle as she reached to help prop her upright again.

"Cole left town years ago and hasn't been back," Jackie explained. "He didn't even attend his daddy's wedding in Indigo Bay last June. Nobody knows why. Except maybe Levi. And he ain't telling a soul."

An AWOL brother. A remarried father. And his mother had left the ranch. Levi Wylder had family secrets. Somehow that made him all the more human, and all the more intriguing.

"Was it over a woman?" Laura asked in a low voice, aware of how busy the diner was today.

"It's always a woman," Mrs. Fisher said with a roll of her eyes as she trotted past. She was obviously up on the Wylder gossip.

The phone on the wall rang and she picked it up on her way by. "Longhorn Diner. No, no. This Greg? Honey, you want 2-2-8-9, but you dialed 2-2-9-9. Okay. Have a lovely day. Pie's on special today if you get a hankering. Oh, and tell MayBeth the book club is moving to Thursdays. The library will be closed on Friday nights from now on... Yes, budget cuts."

"So why the Wylder brothers?" Laura asked Jackie, feeling as though she might already know the answer. She had a bit of a soft spot for the eldest one, which wasn't something she had expected now that they were both adults and living very different lives. But there was something so solid and reliable about the man, and the way that he looked at her... Well, she had to admit her type had changed over the past few days to include men like him.

"I really shouldn't gossip," Jackie said.

"Then don't." Mrs. Fisher pinched her lips together as she

walked by with an order from the kitchen. The phone rang again, and she sighed and tucked the receiver between her ear and shoulder, balancing a stack of plates up her arm.

Jackie gave her a sassy look and flicked her own voluminous hair behind her shoulders. "It's not really gossip," she said as she pressed a finely manicured hand against her checkered blouse, lowering her voice. "Most local men have been snapped up. But those five Wylder boys? They're just…"

Laura waited for her to fill in the blank before she added a few adjectives of her own, such as *wonderful, funny, kind, caring* and *sexy*.

Jackie shook her head again as though refocusing. "They're all dreamy in their unique little ways." She rested her chin on her hand and let out a sigh that Laura unconsciously echoed. She knew exactly what Jackie meant.

"You'd think you two were thirteen with your first crush, the way you're sitting there mooning," Mrs. Fisher said, as she dumped a stack of empty dessert plates into a gray dish bin.

Laura felt her face heat. She'd been thirteen when she'd had her real first crush—on Levi Wylder.

"You're staying at Luanne's?" Jackie asked Laura.

She nodded.

"I'll pick you up at six fifteen. We want to get good seats." She eyed her from head to toe and added, "Wear something cute. Short skirt, tight shirt." She leaned in and whispered, "We might just snag us a few Wylders tonight." She left a few bills on the counter for her coffee, then slid off her stool and headed out, waving and calling hellos to the folks she knew.

Mrs. Fisher picked up Jackie's money and empty cup, while warning, "Be careful. That girl will have you knocked up and married off before you even know the man's middle name."

Laura had been taking a sip of her coffee and nearly choked.

"I'm not joking," Mrs. Fisher said primly. "She's taken about a half-dozen girls to the game, and each of them has ended up in the family way or engaged within a month."

The phone rang yet again and she snatched it, hooking it between her shoulder and ear. "Longhorn Diner. William? No. The note says to turn on the oven *before* I get home. Not now. Well, do you want your supper warm or not? It's game night."

"Were you two talking about Jackie?" Another woman slid onto the newly vacated stool. Broad and strong, she wore dangling feather earrings, broken-in boots and jeans, and carried herself like she could take care of anything and everyone without a second thought. If you needed someone to lean on in town, this was who you would call, Laura suspected.

She nodded and the woman smiled fondly, shaking her head. "She has persistence. I've always liked how she knows what she wants and isn't afraid to go after it."

Mrs. Fisher had finished her phone call, looking slightly miffed. She brushed it off quickly as she said, "Jackie might just catch one of those boys some day, you know."

The newcomer smiled again.

Laura wasn't so sure she wanted to go to the game any longer.

"Can I get a bran muffin, please?" the woman asked.

"Don't you have about forty dozen muffins already baked and stored in your freezer?" Mrs. Fisher asked pointedly.

"I haven't been baking that much." Her reply was good-natured, delivered with a brief, dismissive wave.

"Pie's on special today."

"Auction day," the woman said lightly. She gave a slight head shake and Mrs. Fisher put a muffin in front of her before hustling off to tend to her tables. The woman took a bite, then turned to Laura, who was rummaging through her purse for cash so she could head home, and hopefully come up with a reason to be busy at six fifteen so she didn't find herself adding to Jackie's tally.

"You must be Laura Oakes," the woman stated.

She nodded. "I'm sorry, I don't believe we've met."

"Just in passing at Luanne's funeral. I was helping with the sandwiches." Laura didn't recall. In fact, she couldn't remember much about that hot July day. She'd flown in on an overnight flight from Honduras where she'd been on a photo shoot. She'd attended the funeral, still in shock at her great-aunt's sudden departure, and had then flown back to Honduras that very night, even before the will was read.

"Luanne had a lot of stuff," the woman added. "If you need any help, be sure to call." As though realizing she hadn't introduced herself yet, she put out her hand and said, "I'm Maria Wylder."

"Related to Levi, by chance?"

The woman smiled with what could only be described as affection. "I'm his mother."

Laura quickly replayed everything she and Jackie had said about the hot Wylder boys before Maria arrived. Deciding she hadn't likely overheard anything too embarrassing, Laura relaxed. "Lovely to meet you," she said. "I'm helping out at the riding stable."

Maria's brows pinched with sympathy. "Poor Betty. It's such a shame what her family is going through right now. Especially with her daughter in the middle of filming a movie. Janet's an actress." She raised her voice to Mrs. Fisher, who was putting on a fresh pot of coffee. "Any word on how Betty's son-in-law is doing?"

The waitress shook her head. "No news since Wednesday."

A man with a full head of white hair a little farther down the line of stools stood, dropping bills on the counter. He said to Mrs. Fisher, "I heard he's going to live."

"Of course he is," she replied indignantly. "I've been praying." She walked over and lifted the money he'd set down. "Garfield, honey, you only had a coffee. You've left too much again."

"It's a tip."

She handed him some of the bills. "It's too much for just coffee."

He took her outstretched hand, leaning over the counter so he could kiss it, then looked up at her with a smile that made his face crease with happiness. "Maybe I don't come here for the coffee."

Mrs. Fisher looked part peeved, part delighted as she pulled her hand away. "You're an old scallywag. You know that?"

"You remind me every week."

They laughed, making Laura smile. This diner might be her favorite eatery on Earth.

"Well, hopefully everything's all right in California," Mrs. Wylder said, lightly clearing her throat in an attempt to mask a smile at Garfield Goodwin's flirting. She shifted her attention back to Laura. "Thanks for helping Levi. He tends to take everything on as his own problem, and you've likely saved him a lot of stress. I've heard nothing but good things about the work you're doing and the scholarship you found."

"Thank you." Laura looked away, certain the woman was in the process of figuring out that Laura had made up the scholarship. "That's nice to hear."

Laura placed her money on the counter as an idea came to her. Maria had a freezer full of muffins, and Levi was looking for someone to take care of meals at the ranch... Would it be wrong to drop a hint?

"He asked me to do some cooking out there, too," she stated casually.

"Oh? You cook?"

"Not really. I guess he's desperate." She toyed with her cup, unsure how direct she could be with Maria. Fairly direct, except when it came to telling her how to deal with her own family. There was probably a perfectly good reason she wasn't cooking for the crew.

"Must be mighty desperate," a man grumbled, taking the seat

on the other side of Maria. Likely approaching his seventies, he had flyaway salt-and-pepper hair circling a bald spot, and a small paunch that folded over his large belt buckle. "Taking on a fashion model to run horses. Looking for a legal battle, is he?"

"Oh, Henry," Maria said with thinly disguised exasperation. "Don't be like that."

"I'm only being truthful." His murky gaze focused on Laura. "What do you know about horses, little miss?"

She opened her mouth to admit her faults, but Maria said firmly, "Enough to be helpful and step in during a crisis. I don't see you out there helping Levi, despite the way you talk about family and being there for each other."

Henry harrumphed, his pale cheeks reddening as he pushed away from the counter again. Once he was gone, Maria said to Laura, "Don't mind him. He's an ornery old coot. I didn't mind losing *him* when I divorced his nephew."

"You know, Maria. Those boys of yours are looking mighty skinny despite knowing my daily specials," Mrs. Fisher said, leaning against the counter. Unspoken messages passed between the two older women, and Laura decided the seed had been planted and it was time for her to butt out.

"Are you going to the game tonight?" Maria asked, turning to her before she could escape.

"Apparently I'm in need of knocking up." When the women gave her a silent look, eyebrows raised, Laura added, "Jackie thinks so. I mean, the rumor about her taking friends to the game to meet guys…" She gave a gusty sigh and said, "I think I'll stay home tonight."

Levi's mom snorted in amusement, her eyes crinkling. "You be careful if you change your mind. Jackie's got a verified talent."

"Are you two going to the game?" Laura asked, wishing her face would stop burning.

"The whole town goes, honey," Maria said. "And I wouldn't

miss watching even one game. My boys are going to coach their team to the state championship this year. I can feel it."

"That's right. They are," Mrs. Fisher said firmly.

Their confidence left no doubt in Laura's mind that they were speaking what they felt was the truth. She just hoped they were wrong when it came to Jackie's gift for getting her friends hooked up and in the family way.

LEVI WAS SITTING in a sea of fans, all dressed in red and white, in the tall stands on the home team's side, staring out at the football field. Brant was to his left, the aisle to his right, just the way Levi liked it. His brother was wearing his gaudy red straw cowboy hat, a game tradition, and Levi a white T-shirt with a red checkered shirt overtop, the sleeves rolled up to keep him cool as the hot September sun dipped toward the horizon.

Their mom moved up the bleachers toward the spot their family had always staked out as theirs before the divorce, giving her sons a wave before taking a seat a few rows in front of them. She squeezed in with Daisy-Mae Ray, Jenny Oliver and Mrs. Fisher, the latter of whom had added red plastic flowers to her straw-colored teased hair. She was waving red-and-white pompoms, not unlike the cheerleaders who were warming up at the end of the field near the locker room entrance.

After spotting his mother, Levi unconsciously began scanning the spectators for his father and his new wife, Sophia. Sure enough, they were down near the center line, sharing a hot dog in what was now their seat in the bleachers. Levi wondered for a half second if he had somehow taken a side in the divorce by keeping to Wylder tradition. The thing was, sitting anywhere else just felt plain wrong.

Half the town was out for the game, and despite the start time being several hours past closing for most of the local businesses, many windows had been sporting Gone to the Game signs when Levi had driven by. The stands were filling quickly on what was going to be a big night, as two longstanding rivals went head to head, and the line to the concession stand already wound through the center field's exit chute. Everything was as it should be, and yet Levi couldn't shake the feeling that something was missing.

"Hungry?" Brant asked, standing.

"The line's long."

"April's working tonight. It'll move fast."

Levi dug into his pocket to fish a twenty from his wallet, his stomach grumbling in anticipation.

"The usual?" His brother fisted the bill.

He nodded. "Say hi to April for me." April MacFarlane, a few years younger than Levi, had grown up with them on the ranch, her father having been a long-time hired hand before shifting to something easier on his back when April graduated from high school. She now lived out of town with her husband and four-year-old son, Kurt. She and Levi had barely seen each other over the past few years, but lately she'd been popping into town more, likely due to the ease of getting around now that Kurt was getting a tad bit more independent.

Levi's stomach rumbled again and he glanced toward their mom, Laura's suggestion about asking her to return to the ranch coming to mind. But seeing her laughing with Mrs. Fisher and a few other women from the book club she'd never had time to join until now, he couldn't find it in his heart to ask her to give it up just because their mealtimes were lacking compared to what they'd once been.

"Well, hello," Brant said as he stepped to the aisle, his tone causing Levi to follow his brother's gaze.

Brant was beckoning to Laura and Jackie, encouraging them to climb up the stand to where Levi was sitting. "Two seats here," he called.

Levi stood, trying to hide the goofy smile he couldn't seem to wipe off his face as Laura followed Jackie, paying special attention to where she placed her feet. She was wearing white cowboy boots, a denim miniskirt and a white T-shirt that had most of the men nearby checking her out, Levi noted. No cardinal red, though. Hadn't Jackie clued her in? He eyed Laura's hands, waiting for the flash of ruby-red nails that would help her claim she was indeed sporting the team's colors. But they were now a pale pink, and shorter. She'd also let her hair down, in flaxen waves curling over her shoulders. She looked gorgeous, and every step she took made her hips sway, shifting his heartbeat to double time.

"I didn't know you liked football," he said, as he stepped into the aisle beside Brant, clearing the way to the empty bench beyond.

She smiled as her dark eyes met his. "I usually watch baseball, but football will do in a pinch." She winked and he nearly forgot why he was here, until Jackie bumped into him as she squeezed past in turn.

"Yankees fan?" he asked Laura.

"How'd you know?"

"You were wearing their ball cap on Monday." He was still smiling, unable to care that he likely looked a bit smitten.

"Observant. A good trait in a man," Laura said with another wink. She had taken a seat on the long metal bench, Jackie sliding in beside her. Laura waved at a few people who recognized her, her other hand raised to block the setting sun.

"I'm heading to the concession," Brant announced. "What would you gals like?"

Levi settled beside Jackie, wishing he'd thought to slip in between the women so he could sit by Laura. Jackie shifted suddenly, her hip hitting his as she leaned into his personal space and said authoritatively, "We're fine, Brant. Thanks!"

"I'll be back. Save my seat." Brant hustled down the steps, not making it very far before someone stopped him to chat. Not long after that he paused again, this time to talk with their father and stepmother. Brant pointed up to where Levi was sitting, but Levi knew his dad wouldn't turn to look, and that he wouldn't make his way to their section because it would mean entering his ex-wife's territory.

Levi's stomach rumbled again. At this rate he figured he'd be lucky if there were any hot dogs left by the time Brant made it to the front of the line.

"Beautiful night," Jackie said, her chin and eyes downcast just enough they didn't hide quite under the brim of her cowboy hat as she looked at him through her eyelashes. Full flirt mode.

"Yup." He glanced at Laura's knees, revealed by her miniskirt. They appeared to be almost healed after her tumble into the ditch last weekend. "How are the knees?"

"Much better."

The school band took to the turf, along with the cheerleaders, who tumbled and moved to the music. Their manager, Karen Hartley, was at the sidelines, her head nodding to the beat while the team ran through what looked like a new routine.

"Did you know Karen and I joined the mixed golf league this year?" Jackie said. "She's not very sporty, but she's hoping to date a golfer. There are lots of *handsome* men on the course."

"That's good."

Everyone stood for the national anthem, and Levi took off his white hat, holding it over his heart. When he looked her way, he noticed that Laura was singing with everything she had. He smiled and added more volume to his own voice.

"I didn't know you could sing," Jackie said when they sat down again. "I thought only Cole did."

"Just for the anthem, and in my truck when nobody's around but me and Lupe."

"Is your dog named Lupe as in the French word for wolf?" Laura asked.

"It's short for Guadalupe, because he was pulled out of the Guadalupe River. He's a rescue. Literally."

Brant returned as the game started, carrying a box of food and drinks, enough for all of them. He edged past Levi, then the gals, sitting on the far side of Laura. His brother began idly chatting while handing drinks and hot dogs down to everyone.

"Thank you, Brant," Jackie said. "You shouldn't have."

"How much do I owe you?" Laura asked, squinting as the sun dropped farther in the sky. Levi should have chosen a spot on the other side of the field, even though it tended to get chilly once the sun set and the Wylders never sat there. He had a blanket in his truck, though. Maybe he could pull his brother's trick and slide in next to someone and share its warmth. He was about to suggest they move to the other side of the stadium when his brother dropped his red cowboy hat on Laura's head.

"You owe me not a thing, my dear. It's my treat." He adjusted the hat's brim so it shielded Laura's eyes. "Now you're wearing the team colors."

"Oh, Brant. You're such a sweetheart," Jackie chirped.

Brant took a big bite of his hot dog, and Levi noted that Laura left the hat on, looking more a cowgirl than she had a right to.

The game continued, and every once in a while he could hear Myles hollering to the players on the field, telling them to protect, run, and pull their head out of their butts, among other things, which caused the spectators within earshot to chuckle.

"Is he always like that?" Laura asked Brant, pointing to Myles.

"Oh, yeah. He gets into it. And so does Ryan. He's just quieter."

"You think they'll make state this year?"

Brant immediately shushed her. "This is not a topic open for debate." He glanced around as though she'd said something dangerous, causing her to laugh. "Only God is bigger than Football around here."

Jackie pressed her shoulder against Levi's. "Are you going to the next barn dance?"

He gave a noncommittal grunt, and Brant leaned across the women to say, "You should go."

"Pretty sure I'm going to be busy that day."

"You don't dance?" Laura asked. Her voice was sweet, curious.

"He can dance up a storm. He just doesn't. Most women can't keep up." Brant had finished his hot dog and was eyeing Jackie's. "You gonna eat that?"

She held it protectively against her chest before giving him a flirty smile and offering it to him like it was something special, her shoulder leaving Levi's in the process. He shifted farther to his right, the metal bleacher seat chilling him briefly.

"Levi can get me another hot dog, right, Levi?" Jackie gave his knee a squeeze and he jumped.

"Uh, sure." He was fairly certain she didn't want one.

"Us girls will be at the dance," Jackie said, "and looking for partners. Laura and Brant can dance together, and you and I can tear up the floor. What do you say?"

Levi noticed that Laura had focused her attention on picking at a corner of her hot dog bun.

"You going, Laura?" he asked. "Or will you be back in New York by then?

"Spend a bit more time here enjoying fresh air and hot cowboys," Jackie pleaded.

Laura smiled weakly. "I didn't make much progress this week, so chances are I'll still be here for some fresh air and cowboys." There was that cloud of worry chasing the smile off her face again.

"Hot cowboys," Jackie corrected.

"Need any help?" Brant asked, his tone brotherly, kind.

"You're busy," Levi found himself saying.

"I was going to offer you," he replied with a wink.

"It's mostly stuff I have to deal with personally. Alone." Laura was still picking at the bun, a far-off look in her eyes. Levi once again wished Jackie wasn't sitting between them, and that he knew Laura well enough that he could reassure her.

He couldn't imagine what it would feel like if the tabloids were making things up about him as they were with her. He'd gone online and done some searching after she'd left the other day, and what they were saying about her wasn't kind. Then again, kindness wasn't what a lot of those sites seemed to be known for.

The spectators around them jumped to their feet, and Levi realized he'd missed seeing the play. He checked the scoreboard. The Torpedoes were ahead by two touchdowns, both of which he'd missed.

By halftime the sun had set, the bright lights were flooding the stadium and he was feeling antsy, unable to focus. He stood. "Want to go stretch your legs?" he asked Laura. Maybe a walk and talk would make her smile.

Jackie jumped to her feet. "Great idea. These seats are so hard." She made a show of rubbing the back of her skirt.

"I'm okay, thanks," Laura said. She remained where she was, and behind her Brant gave a shrug.

Unable to think of a reason to retract his offer, Levi found himself going for a walk with the wrong woman.

LAURA NEEDED TO GET A GRIP. She was tensing up as though Mrs. Fisher's prediction about Jackie getting her involved with someone at the game was fact, not local lore.

Jackie was endearing, someone Laura already considered a friend, even though it was apparent she was friends with everyone, judging by all the hellos and hugs she'd given out while making their way up to these seats with the Wylders. As soon as she'd arrived at Laura's, she'd taken one look at her and declared she needed to wear something different to the game. Laura's silk tank top was traded for the form-fitting white T-shirt she slept in. Her ponytail was shucked, Jackie doing a better and faster job of teasing out her loose curls than many of the experts she'd worked with on photo shoots. Her makeup was touched up in a way that made her new tan look fresh, healthy and slightly dewy. Next, since her capris and gold sandals were declared inappropriate, the two of them raced to Blue Tumbleweed, begging the owner Jenny to stay open a few minutes longer while Jackie tracked down the perfect denim skirt and a pair of white cowboy boots. Declared lethally gorgeous at last, Laura went off with her to the game.

Now, looking around the bleachers, she noted that Jackie hadn't steered her wrong. She appeared to belong, other than her absence of red—an oversight Laura figured must have been intentional when she caught Jackie's satisfied smile after Brant plunked his red hat on her head. Too bad Levi hadn't been wearing a red hat she could have borrowed.

She gave herself a little shake. What was she thinking? Even though he was cute, sweet and all of that, she knew Jackie wanted Levi for herself. Sadly for her new friend, it didn't look as though Levi was returning her interest.

Mrs. Fisher turned to wave, and Levi's mom, as well. Laura waved back, feeling welcome, something she realized she'd been in desperate need of lately. Here in Sweetheart Creek there were no tabloid rumors making people glance at her twice. There was no need to hide out at home when she got a pimple, or to prove she was the most gorgeous woman in the room. She could just... breathe and be herself, and be accepted. She loved it.

"You're not in a hurry to sell Luanne's house?" Brant asked, breaking into her thoughts. "There's nothing pushing you to rush back home?"

She scanned the crowd, looking for Levi and Jackie. "I'm sure everything will click into place when it needs to," she said absently, not wanting to think about how she feared that selling the house would leave her feeling completely adrift, or how much she wanted to stay in town for much longer than her earmarked few weeks.

"The right offer hasn't come in yet?" he asked. Brant was a kind, gentle soul, and she could tell why he had a thriving veterinarian business. He was the type of man you immediately trusted, and if you weren't careful you'd find yourself pouring your heart out to him.

"Not yet," she replied.

"It's nice you don't have to leave right away."

Despite her caution, she found herself saying, "There isn't much for me to go back to." Except for her sister, but Ava traveled for her job as a location scout for commercials, music videos and movies to the point that she was rarely in the city. "The people I used to hang out with aren't as interested in spending time with me now that I'm no longer a model."

"Seriously?" Brant asked, his eyebrows raised in disbelief.

Before he could say it, she did. "Apparently I didn't choose true friends. Or a worthy boyfriend, either."

Brant was quiet for a long moment. "I imagine it would be difficult to know how genuine someone is when you have a certain level of fame."

"Yeah," Laura said, awkwardly brushing at the tears that sprang to her eyes. She wasn't used to having shorter fingernails. That afternoon she'd walked into the Big Hair Salon and had her gel nails filed down to a more reasonable length for working with horses. Still gorgeous, just more practical. She'd also had the color changed to something more honest, reflective of how she wanted to feel—calm, feminine and pretty.

"I guess now's not a good time," Brant said, "to tell you I'm only being nice because I find you beautiful."

Laura didn't breathe for a second, then burst out laughing. She scowled playfully. "I don't like you. Not at all."

Brant laughed as well, the corners of his eyes creasing. "Are you allergic to dogs?"

"Is that how veterinarians propose?"

He shook his head as though in disbelief. "You know, just because I'm handsome and good with animals, women take innocent questions and turn them into marriage proposals."

She laughed again, feeling lighter than she had all day. There was something about him that caused her to let go of her worries. Kind of like when she was with Levi, but without the butterflies-in-her-stomach effect. She caught movement out of the corner of her eye and looked up to find the eldest Wylder brother inhaling through his nostrils, his glare locked on Brant as Jackie slid onto the bench.

Laura edged over to make room for the new arrivals, but Brant grasped her elbow, holding her in place. "Can you grab me another soda?"

Before she could protest, he had her on her feet and standing in the aisle. She blinked, not quite believing she had been hoisted from her seat by Brant and sent on an errand. Shaking her head, Laura walked slowly to the concession stand, wondering if she should just keep going.

When she returned, she saw that he was seated by the aisle, Levi to his left. Brant stood, lifting the borrowed hat from her head and plunking it on his own. Taking the drink, he scooted past her, excusing himself, and walked down the steps, handing the soda to his mother when he reached her. Maria looked delighted.

"Always the suck-up," Levi muttered.

"He is thoughtful," Laura said, settling beside Levi and trying to sort out what had happened.

"He is *very* thoughtful," Jackie agreed, her lips curved in a soft smile. "Like Cole and you." Her voice warmed. "It must run in the family."

Levi stared out at the field where the game was resuming, and adjusted his white cowboy hat with a jerk. For a moment Laura was tempted to flirt, to steal it and plunk it on her own head. But she had a feeling he wasn't in the mood for horseplay, and that Jackie wouldn't appreciate her focusing her attention on a man she was interested in.

Laura closed her eyes, visualizing her troubles washing past her like driftwood in a river. They weren't real problems. They were nothing but hiccups, kind of like her mini crush on Levi.

7

*After the game, Levi left the stands with Jackie and Laura. As they walked down the steps, which had no railing, he took Laura's elbow, well aware of the curious onlookers. He couldn't help it. Somewhere along the line he had called dibs despite the poor timing of his interest, and he wanted the entire town to know—including Brant. If anyone was going to be considered by Laura, it was going to be him.

The problem was, even if her flirting meant more than simple fun, she wasn't staying. He'd already learned the hard way that women who loved the limelight didn't return to Sweetheart Creek, and that he wasn't cut out for long-distance relationships. He wanted his girlfriend here with him, enjoying life and each new day. And that didn't look like Laura's future, from what he could tell.

And what game had Brant been playing, setting his hat on Laura's head? Had he been tossing his gauntlet into the ring as well? Had his offer to purchase Luanne's house been a gesture Levi didn't understand? If so, it made no sense, as him buying the property would send Laura home.

Laura received a lot of nods and greetings as they passed,

making Levi realize she'd had a busy week in town. Everyone from Mrs. Fisher to April MacFarlane and Kurt, who'd been hanging out at the concession stand with his mom. The welcoming smiles and hellos warmed his heart more than he figured they should. But she'd said she was hoping lightning would strike twice in this town and help her out, and he'd long ago learned you had to be careful what you wished for.

Levi cleared his throat, trying to figure out a way to convince Laura to take longer with her aunt's house. A lot longer.

Behind him, he heard shuffling, stumbling footsteps, then felt hands landing on his back, followed by a giggle as Jackie hugged him from behind. "Oops!"

He turned to ensure she was okay. By the time he had Jackie righted and himself extracted, Laura was in the parking lot standing near Brant's truck under a streetlight, a small brown-and-black dog in her arms.

"Who's this?" he asked, joining them along with Jackie. He ruffled the dog's furry ears and was rewarded by its teeth grabbing the rolled-up sleeve of his shirt.

"This is Target," Brant said.

"Cutest little dog ever," Laura said, with a big, dopey smile that made him want to give her an entire litter of pups.

"Target?" he repeated. Brant fulfilled the animal control contract for the county, and often took in lost, abandoned or injured animals. So far his brother had given pretty much everyone close to him a dog. Levi had Lupe, Myles had Buckey—short for Bucket, an object stuck on the dog's head when she was found—and Ryan had Joey, named after Trader Joe's, since the dog had been found by the owner of the grocery store. Even Carmichael and Jackie had been given dogs to foster, which they'd also ended up adopting, like Levi had.

It made sense that if Brant was working something behind the scenes he'd give Laura a dog, too. But again, that didn't compute with buying her house. Brant also wasn't one to hone in on another man's interests, and he knew Levi had called dibs even before he'd realized it himself.

But...Laura. She was the kind of woman men fought for. And not just because she was easy on the eyes. She was smart, helpful and fun.

However, the little comments and looks from his brother made Levi feel as though Brant might be trying to act as a wingman to him. Yet his actions didn't line up to being a good one.

Either way, not getting to know Laura better would be a missed opportunity.

"Found him in the Target parking lot," Brant said, interrupting Levi's thoughts. "Judging by his rough coat and black snout he looks like he's got some border terrier in him."

"Some people," Jackie said with a shake of her head.

"Nobody's claimed him, and he doesn't get along with Dodge," Brant added.

Levi narrowed his eyes. Brant's dog, which had been found roaming around the local Dodge dealership, got along with everyone, kind of like Brant himself. And this dog, if it was indeed a border terrier, would be a charming escape artist who'd probably adopt one person and shadow him or her forever. It was an interesting choice for Laura.

Jackie was sucking in her cheeks, trying not to release a smile that might tip off Laura as to Brant's plans. "I think I'll go see what Ryan is up to," she said, striding across the parking lot and back to the field, where the youngest Wylder was likely having a post-game meeting with the team.

"What will you do with Target?" Laura asked Brant.

"Usually I'd have someone foster him."

"Why's that?" Levi asked, deciding to be his brother's wingman in what was surely his give-Laura-a-dog plan. Anything that might keep her in Texas a little longer worked for him.

"A puppy deserves to be with a family, to have green grass under his paws and get lots of love. This guy needs some training and discipline, and he won't get it sitting in a kennel in the back of my clinic until I can find someone to take him in." Brant reached out and ruffled Target's nape, his expression sad and resigned to the fate he was going to give the pup.

"Can't you take him?" Laura asked, turning the puppy toward Levi.

He shook his head. "Too small." Too clever. Too much work.

"But he's so cute!"

"He's likely to find out the hard way that horses have mighty big feet, and that his puppy games aren't appreciated." Levi gave a shrug, trying to resist the sad look Laura was giving him. A look that made him want to be a hero and take the puppy. "I don't have the time right now to get Target where he needs to be, training-wise, so he can safely roam the ranch unattended."

Laura's eyebrows were arched, her eyes big, and he felt himself caving.

"What's this?" Levi's mom asked, coming to join them.

"A puppy in need of a home," Levi said, stepping back. His mother reached for the little animal. So far she'd managed to avoid being given a dog to foster, likely due to the no-pets policy of her in-town rental. Midreach she caught Brant's expression and dropped her arms, tipping her head to the side, making a soft sound instead.

"Cute little thing," she said. "Levi, are you doing anything for your birthday?"

"I haven't thought about it," he replied truthfully.

"When's your birthday?" Laura asked.

"Wednesday."

There was a warmth in Laura's gaze, and he wondered if she would help him celebrate. Maybe dinner out, with a slice of cake afterward? An intimate affair that didn't include his annoying brothers.

"Turning thirty-five," Maria said. She gave his cheek an affectionate pat, saying, "How did I get a son this old?"

"I'm only thirty-one," Brant said, straightening his shoulders.

"You should have a party," Laura exclaimed. Her eyes had a slightly dreamy look, and Levi could tell she had something in mind. "You've got that amazing patio out back. It would be perfect for entertaining." Her smile was as open as it had been when she'd been chatting with Brant during the game, and Levi quickly found himself agreeing.

"Did someone say party?" Ryan asked, joining them.

"Levi's having one." Brant said.

"But don't you have ranching work to do, not to mention being important and busy?" Ryan teased.

"Ryan, this is Laura," Levi said, making the introduction. "Laura, the youngest of the Wylder brothers."

"Congratulations on the win tonight," she said.

"Thanks." He flashed a smile.

"I think a gathering is a great idea," Maria said. "I worry about you being isolated on that ranch and not getting out enough."

She frowned at something across the parking lot and Levi followed her gaze. Myles was standing with the cheerleader's manager, Karen Hartly, his movements awkward as he tried to help her put a large bag of pompoms in the trunk of her small car. He looked like a teenager with his first crush, all arms and legs, completely uncoordinated, which was not like him.

"She is so out of his league," Ryan muttered, watching Myles with a wince. "Like, come on? A librarian? For *Myles*? And hasn't he figured out women just love you, then leave you?"

"You're never going to find that perfect ranch wife while sitting around at home," Brant joked, bringing Levi's attention back to the present conversation.

He moved closer to Laura, worried about where his brother was going with his teasing.

"And what would this perfect ranch wife look like?" she asked, picking up on the topic.

"She'd be easy to get along with," Levi muttered, giving his brother a sharp glance. "Helpful around the ranch." And she'd make him want to smile, making each new day something to look forward to.

"Simply perfect. Like Levi," Brant said sweetly.

"She'll muck out the stables, and put her back into every task," Ryan added. "The two of them won't even have to have conversations, because they'll read each other's thoughts." He folded his hands under his chin and batted his eyelashes at Levi.

"I'm glad you finally admitted I'm perfect," Levi said, crossing his arms.

"So about this party?" their mother prompted with a sigh. "Will you have it on Wednesday night?"

Levi shrugged. On the ranch pretty much every day of the week was the same, just that on Sundays you couldn't zip into town to replace a part due to stores being closed. "May as well."

"Are you going to feed everybody steak?" Brant asked. "Because I'm tired of it."

"Who said you're invited?" Levi retorted.

"Of course I'm invited." Brant crossed his own arms, imitating Levi's stance. "You have to invite family. All of us."

Even their great-uncle Henry, their dad and Sophia? That sounded like a recipe for disaster.

Ryan folded his arms in turn and nodded. Levi caught Laura smirking at the brotherly banter.

"Which means you should also invite April and her family," Brant said.

"Of course," Levi agreed. "She's practically a Wylder." He said in an aside to Laura, "Her dad was a ranch hand. She grew up with us."

"Poor gal," Laura said with a teasing smile.

"It's not public knowledge..." Maria said, lowering her voice.

Everyone instinctively stepped closer, forming a circle around her. "...but it sounds like her marriage is going through a rough spot. So go easy on her."

"Always," Levi said. Everyone nodded, and stepped back.

"I can help with food for the party," Laura offered.

"That would be great," Maria said.

As they discussed details, Levi wondered what was it about Laura that made him feel as though she was the one he'd been waiting for, and that if he moved too fast he'd lose her. But that if he didn't move fast enough, she'd slip away...

LAURA CONTINUED to cuddle the puppy in her arms while the football field's parking lot emptied out, people either walking the few blocks home or climbing into their pickups.

The idea of entertaining in the Wylders' big house with that wonderful stone patio had her excited. *And* she was going to Levi's birthday party. The man deserved a bit of pampering given all the weight he seemed to carry for his family. Honestly, she wasn't sure which she was more excited about—getting a chance to put on the shindig or to spoil him a little.

"Levi, do you have time to help me secure my bookshelf to the wall tonight?" Mrs. Wylder asked, jangling her keychain and taking a few steps away from the group as though preparing to leave. "I'm going to be babysitting Kurt next week and I'm worried he'll try to climb it."

Levi glanced from Laura to his brother before reluctantly nodding. "I ordered a new air filter for your car, too, Mom. I figured it was due, and Clint'll charge you through the nose to change it out."

"You're a good man," she said, giving him an affectionate smile. Then she tugged at the longish hair around his ears, eyebrows raised.

"I know," he muttered. "Haircut. It's on the list."

"And you know if you're too busy with the ranch, Clint said he'd pop by the house and swap that filter out for me."

"He did?" Levi's eyes narrowed, and Laura adored how his protective side included his mother. It made Laura want to dream up something so he'd come by and help her out, too. Maybe kiss her.

That crush was never going to go away, was it?

"He does that for everyone in town," Maria said, in a tone that was both amused and soothing.

"I don't think he does." Levi frowned at Brant. "Does he do that for you?"

His brother shrugged. "I take care of my own stuff."

Levi didn't seem entirely convinced as he began to walk away with his mother. He paused, looking at the puppy dozing in Laura's arms, then at her. "If you need anything, shoot me a text."

"What would I need?" Laura grinned at him. "An oil change?"

Ryan and Brant laughed, while Levi scowled halfheartedly before a smile managed to break loose. She loved the way his eyes sparkled when he smiled. He was a handsome man. A good one, too.

"I gotta run. Nice meeting you," Ryan said, heading toward Myles, who had reappeared across the parking lot with Jackie.

As he went, Henry, the cranky old man from the diner, called out to him, "What was your quarterback's problem tonight? We want to go to state!"

"He's a kid. He's allowed bad days. Give him a break," Ryan called back.

"And that's why you'll never make it to the championship game!"

"He's a fun man," Brant mumbled under his breath, and Laura gave a half laugh of agreement. "You've had the pleasure of meeting Sweetheart Creek's welcoming committee, I presume?"

He turned his back to Henry, and Laura shifted as well. Brant was a little shorter than her, she noted, which wasn't atypical, seeing as she was over six feet.

"I met him today. It was…lovely."

Brant smiled. "Sorry."

"Not your fault, I'm sure," she said, as she passed him the puppy. Jackie was moving toward her sports car, and Laura worried that she might leave her behind.

"Well, he is related—he's my grandfather's brother—so I feel the need to apologize for his…everything." Brant cuddled the puppy in his arms, his red hat dipping as he blew gently on its head, causing it to twist and roll, tongue hanging out, ready to play. "If you hear of someone who can take this guy for a few days, let me know. It breaks my heart having him in the kennel when he could be in someone's home."

Laura had turned to catch up with Jackie, but slowed her steps. "What does it take to foster a dog?"

"Do you know much about puppies?"

"I have time to learn." She sucked in a breath. Wait. Was she really considering taking in a puppy just because it was adorable and had snuggled in her arms like it belonged there? "Well, if he'd be okay alone for a few hours when I go to the ranch to work with the riders."

"He'd be fine in his kennel for that long. He's active, but he also needs naps to recharge. I have everything you'd require in the truck if you could take him for even one night. It would help so much."

She paused, considering.

"You can call me if there's anything you need," Brant continued. "Here, put your number in my phone." Shifting the pup, he pulled his cell from his back pocket and handed it to her, and she added her number. When she started to pass it back he said, "Shoot yourself a text, and then you'll have my number, too."

She sent herself a smiley face, then looked into the big dark eyes of the puppy in Brant's arms. "What do I do about training him to go in the yard?"

"He's partially trained, but I'll give you the booklet I give all foster parents. It'll tell you most of the things you need to know about training, as well as a general idea of what to expect."

Laura held back a grin. A puppy. She'd always wanted a dog, but hadn't felt as though she had the space in the city.

"Okay. I'll take him."

"Great." Brant's smile was open and warm, and reminded her of Levi. As though reading her mind, he added, "And if you can't get ahold of me—that happens when I'm in emergency surgery or have my hand up a cow's—well…" He cleared his throat. "You can always call Levi. He's good with every kind of emergency or problem."

Laura peered at the puppy again so Brant wouldn't notice the blush that crept across her cheeks at the mention of his brother's name. She was already imagining scenarios where she might have to shoot Levi a message. What kind of situation would get him to come over to her place, but not put the dog in danger or make her look like a helpless idiot?

She gave herself a shake. Levi would see right through any ploy and call her on it. Plus he wasn't the type who was in the habit of rescuing damsels.

"I've only ever come across one problem he can't solve," Brant said, handing the puppy back to Laura.

"What's that?" she asked, curious about what could have stumped a man who seemed able to solve pretty much everything.

Brant's expression closed off as he turned to the truck. "Let me grab you the chew toys, leash and food." Moments later, his look serious, he spoke to her through the gap between the door and the frame. "If Target becomes too much, let me know. I don't want to overburden you. You're doing a wonderful thing, but I know how demanding a puppy can be."

Jackie drove up, her nose scrunched as she asked, "Are you taking the dog?"

Laura nodded, her heart filled with warmth.

"I just got my car detailed." She patted the cloth passenger seat. "Brant, be a sweetie and give them a ride home?"

"Of course," he replied.

Jackie lowered the brim of her hat with a satisfied smile and drove off. So this was how she got her friends paired up with men. She ditched them.

Laura slowly turned to Brant. He was a great guy, but if she was going to choose a Wylder, she would prefer someone a little older, and the same height as her. Someone whose name started with an *L*.

8

---

*L*aura stood watching Target zip around the house, taking in everything. Brant had been about to give her a rundown on what to expect with the puppy when he'd been called away to deal with a pig emergency.

She let Target out into the backyard when he began to sniff a corner with a bit too much interest. Luckily, the back porch light illuminated the entire yard, so she could keep tabs on him. Glancing around the grassy expanse, she wondered if anything in the flower beds might be toxic to dogs. She'd already discovered the five-month-old pup liked to chew, but overall, seemed mostly trained. He began chasing a moth, and Laura, after checking both gates on the fence, slipped into the house to grab the booklet Brant had given her.

Target began yelping as soon as the door closed, and Laura clutched the booklet, watching from the window. If she went outside to soothe the puppy, would she be rewarding his behavior? Before she could thumb through for any advice, her phone rang.

Reina. Not an email, but a late night Friday call, which meant her agent needed an immediate answer on something. Sighing internally, Laura clicked on. "Hey, Reina, what's up?"

"Emma Carrington called today. I wanted to tell you earlier but I was in meetings."

"I'm retired," Laura reminded her gently.

"That's right. However, your retainer contract with her All You line doesn't end for another six months."

Laura shut her eyes. She knew that, but had been hoping Emma would let the contract lapse without calling her in. Laura had taken only one retainer contract during her career, because she believed in what Emma was trying to do with her all-natural line of cosmetics and had wanted to support her efforts.

"They have a new line of products and need a few photos."

"Is there any way out of it?" A new product could mean several weeks of work if Emma wanted one of her typical indoor-outdoor shoots. And right now Laura wanted to be here, figuring things out, not putting a halt to them so she could return to the city to chase old dreams.

"There always is, but it will cost you."

"How much?"

"You'll be in direct breach of contract. The kill fee will cost you more than it's worth. I'd do the shoot."

Laura paused a second to mull it over. If Reina said it wasn't worth it, then it wasn't.

"When does she want me?"

"Next week."

That's about when she'd planned to head home to take care of a few things, but somewhere along the line she'd decided to stay on in Sweetheart Creek a lot longer.

"I'm busy."

"You're retired."

"Can you push her off a few weeks?"

"I'll do my best."

As Laura ended the call, the doorbell rang. She flicked on the entry light and opened the door, surprised to find Levi on her steps, still in his game-colored shirts.

"Brant said you could use a rundown on puppies."

Laura couldn't help but smile as she let him in, pleased that Brant had sent her top choice in Wylder brothers.

Levi crouched, still wearing his boots and hat, and made a clicking sound.

"Target's outside." The yelping had stopped, thankfully.

"How's it going so far?"

"He's pretty much stolen my heart. Target—Target has." She felt herself blush as she stumbled over her words.

"Brant's a good judge of who will connect with an animal, that's for sure."

Laura nodded, half distracted by Levi's very presence in her home, so vital and strong. She loved that he was the same height as she was, and even a little taller when he was in boots and she was in her flip-flops. Sexy. Oh, so sexy.

"He's good about investing in his foster parents, too."

"What do you mean?"

Levi just shook his head, not answering her, the same way Brant had acted when she'd asked what problem Levi had been unable to solve.

She reached out and touched Levi's arm. He looked at her hand in surprise before meeting her eyes, and she withdrew, suddenly bashful. She wanted to do a lot more than just reach out and touch him.

"What do you mean, he invests?" she pressed.

"He likes to make sure everybody gets off on the right foot."

She was getting to know Levi well enough to sense he was hiding something. She also knew she could probably push a little and get him to confess to whatever it was. "There's more to this story, Levi Wylder."

His head jerked when he heard his full name, and he watched her with that careful gaze of his. She could tell he liked how she'd called him out. And he was smiling. He had been since the moment he'd walked in the door, and it looked good on him.

"What is Brant really doing with this puppy?"

Levi's body language quieted. "He's testing you."

"Testing me?"

"Yes."

"How?" She crossed her arms, worried that this was some sort of predate exam she was being subjected to, thanks to Jackie subtly pushing them together at the game.

"He thinks you'd give Target a good home."

"The deal is I take him in for one night."

"I started by fostering Lupe for one night, too. Just until he found the right home or another temporary place." He tipped his head. "One night became a couple more, and pretty soon I couldn't part with the dog."

Laura drew herself up, unsure whether she should feel indignant or flattered. "But I'm…maybe leaving. Eventually. He knows that." Her excuse felt weak. She *was* leaving at some point, wasn't she?

Levi peered at her from under the brim of his hat. "But just so you know, he's done this to practically everyone in the family." The way he looked at her and quietly emphasized the word *family* made her feel a crash of emotions. There was something there. A question. An invitation. Something that made her spirit awaken and want to move a little closer, to dig in and discover what exactly was hiding behind those words. But before she could begin to pick apart why she felt that way she heard a panicked yelp from the backyard.

She hustled to the back door, Levi at her elbow. She couldn't see a flash of fur in the yard, so hurried off the small wooden deck and crouched down, looking under it, but the night was too dark for her to see farther than a foot.

"Target!" Levi called. "Here, boy!" Hands on his hips, he

searched the night sky, his expression grim. "Are there birds of prey around here?"

Laura covered her face with her palms. "I'm a horrible foster parent. I've already lost the dog. I didn't even think about birds of prey."

"Let's check the alley," Levi suggested. "We're at that time of night when nocturnal and daytime animals are changing shifts. Target probably found a hole in the fence and slipped out." With long strides, Levi covered the grass to the rear fence, then leaned over it as he looked left and right. "See? There he is."

Laura rushed to the fence just as Levi turned. They crashed into each other, his arms going around her so they wouldn't topple over. Her mind flashed to the wonderful hug he'd given her last week, and for a moment she considered sliding her hands up his red shirt and wrapping her arms around his neck. Instead, she jumped back, feeling embarrassed for wishing for more than his friendship.

She opened the back gate and called Target, who renewed his yelping. The streetlight at the corner cast enough of a glow that she could see him struggling one house down, his collar caught on something near a garbage can. When Levi hurried over, freeing the dog and lifting him into his arms, the pup whimpered happily and licked his face.

"He's going to love you forever," Laura said.

"You're his person," Levi stated. And when he handed the dog to her, she received her own excited greeting.

"I don't think he's very discriminating."

Back in the yard, she set Target down, only to hear Levi shout, "Grab him! We don't know how he got out, and he could be a runner."

Laura scrambled for the dog, but he bolted, darting toward a spot in the fence near the corner. She groaned and returned to the alley, where Target was barking and running in circles like it was all a game.

"You're going to exhaust me, pup."

"Do you have some wire fencing in the garage?" Levi asked, coming up beside her. "We can string some along that corner to keep him in."

"I left some rabbit fencing in the garden shed eons ago. It might still be here."

"I think I remember you buying that," Levi said, with a slow smile that made her heart give an extra thud. "Skunk problems, right?"

She nodded. They were standing close, their gazes locked, the dog still barking and spinning in the alley.

"You always helped me find the right things for every job." Every time.

"But you never accepted my help with the work." Before she could explain her need for independence, he said, "You completed a lot of projects that summer."

"I did." His hand was cupping her elbow, her palms resting against his chest. Behind Levi she could see the lingering results of some of those old projects, as well as spot a few more problems that should be taken care of. Why hadn't she come back each summer—if only for a long weekend—to help her aunt? She'd loved being here.

"You're very independent."

Laura opened her mouth, worried that he would take it personally, like Memphis had. He'd resented her need to work on her career. He'd also resented how hard she worked and the pride she'd taken in her ability to take care of herself financially, even though he'd often bragged about her wealth.

"I like it." Levi was smiling.

Laura relaxed and smiled back. Then, remembering the dog was on the loose, she broke free of the lovely embrace and set to work luring him back into the yard.

Half an hour later, the fence's gaps were securely covered with wire, and Laura and Levi sat on the back step with cold sodas, watching to see if the dog discovered any new escape routes.

As Laura lifted her bottle of root beer to her lips, Levi did the same. Before taking a sip, she tapped it against his and leaned closer. "Cheers. And thanks for the help."

"Any time." He clinked his bottle against hers and looked at her. Crickets chirped, and a frog croaked nearby. Levi didn't shift away, holding her gaze for a long moment. Laura leaned closer, waiting to see if the man she'd always had a crush on would finally press his lips to hers.

LEVI HAD BEEN THINKING about what it would be like to kiss Laura just as she leaned in, her red lips parted as though she was wondering the same.

He waited a beat, reading her body language a second time before giving in to what he'd wanted from the moment he'd seen her standing in the ditch above her broken suitcase in those sexy, impractical heels.

Her lips were warm and soft, and as she moved her mouth, he realized that this was what kissing was supposed to feel like. It was a promise of more to come, of happiness and distraction.

When, reluctantly, he broke the long kiss, Laura's eyes opened slowly, and she tried to hide a shy smile. He was close enough to steal another kiss, so he did. His action was rewarded by her hands bracketing his face to deepen and lengthen the connection. Sitting with her in the glow of the porch light, he began to realize that Laura was the kind of woman who would always keep him on his toes. She might not cause him to check off all the boxes on his list, but when he thought long and hard about it, that list was missing some of the most important things, such as Laura.

He wanted to share his morning view of the pasture with her, to fill her cup with coffee along with his. To stand in silence, admiring the beauty of the morning, savoring kisses and stolen moments. To spend the evenings chatting about their day and their dreams for the future. The feeling hit him so hard he had to stand up in order to breathe.

Laura's eyes widened at his sudden movement, and he saw her red lipstick had smeared. He bent down, quickly placing a kiss on her forehead and leaving a trace of lipstick there.

He wiped his own mouth to erase any traces of red. He needed to get out of here, needed to think. Getting involved with a woman like Laura was not part of his plan, and he was pretty sure he wasn't part of hers, either.

He dropped into a crouch, placing one hand on the step beside her hip, then angling her mouth up toward his for a hard, final kiss.

"I've got to go." *While I still can.*

She seemed too surprised to say anything coherent, and before disappearing around the side of the house, he stopped, turned and asked, "When are you really going back to New York?"

Laura opened her mouth, but nothing other than an aborted sigh broke the silent night. She simply turned her palms upward and shrugged helplessly.

Levi strode back to her, crouching in front of her again and grasping her bare knees. He pulled his hands away, aware of how distracting she was in her cute denim skirt, of how much he wanted her and how much that need could blind him from every thought he should be focusing on right now.

"I have to know," he said, still crouching.

Her eyes cut away. "I'll tell you in enough time that you can find someone to replace me. I won't leave you hanging."

"I'm not worried about the riding program." He'd already dropped his search for Betty's replacement, however unwise that might be. "I need to know because I think I'm falling for you."

Her serious gaze slowly turned back to him.

"You're not part of my plan, Laura. Having a long-distance relationship isn't, either. And neither—" he lowered his voice "—is having my heart broken. I need to know when you're really leaving."

"Aren't you moving a little fast?" She had reached out, was toying with the collar of his red shirt, her fingers moving tentatively.

"Yes."

She gave a shaky, nervous laugh, the pinch between her brows vanishing.

"Some decisions don't require a lot of thought," he said.

"This is a decision?"

He took his thumb and gently rubbed away a lipstick smear left from their kiss. "You need to wear less of this stuff around me. It's obvious what we've been up to."

Her fingers left his shirt and she picked up the bottle of root beer she'd placed on the step between her feet, giving him a look more serious than any he'd seen yet. "What about Jackie?"

It took him a moment to realize what she was asking. "She still has four more Wylders to choose from. She's not particular, and I'm certain I'm not her top pick."

Laura turned her focus to her root beer bottle.

"Well?" he prompted.

"Would it be wrong to say wait and see?"

He stood up, feeling frustrated. Hadn't he just made it clear he didn't want to wait and see? He wanted to know right here, right now what her intentions were.

"Levi," she said, with an edge to her voice. "At the moment I can live wherever I want. We have time to go on some dates, but I am not going to commit to anything before I spend more time with you."

Right. That was practical.

"Fair enough." He reached down and pulled her to her feet. "Let's go."

LAURA LAUGHED when Levi stopped his truck just a few blocks from her house. They'd tucked a tired Target into his kennel, then Levi had led her to his vehicle after requesting she put her boots back on, not saying where they were going or what he had planned.

They were now parked outside the Watering Hole, which looked as though it could have been the first structure ever built in the town. Its wooden siding was weathered like an unpainted barn, without a drop of stain protecting the exterior from the relentless Texas sun. Red neon lettering above the doorway said Tavern, and it had rustic saloon-style doors. The night was cool and a light breeze ruffled Laura's hair as she stepped onto the street. The music coming from the bar was too raw and imperfect to be anything but live.

"What are we doing?" she asked.

"Going on a date," Levi said simply. He came around the front of the truck, catching her hand in his.

She laughed again. This was totally the Levi she was coming to adore. She'd stated she wanted to get to know him better and he'd come up with an immediate solution. A date.

She liked that.

"I am going to crack you like an egg," she said, tapping his chest. "I'm going to find out what's under that shell and get to know every bit of you. Are you ready for that?"

"More than ready," he said, stopping to sweep her into a warm embrace and a lingering kiss that left her breathless.

Kisses like that could quite happily lock her into a life in Sweetheart Creek.

She smiled, while battling a sudden bout of nerves at how quickly they were moving toward more-than-friends.

As they approached the tavern, a dog came sauntering out beneath the half doors, a piece of bread in its mouth.

"Hey, Rusty," Levi said, giving the dog a pat. He said to Laura, "He's a regular. He comes for the leftover cheese bread."

Inside, the place was bustling, a sea of red and white, proving that this was where to hang out after football games. Laura made a mental note to find something red to wear to the next one.

"Is there a game next week?" she asked.

"Away game," he said. "Need a ride?"

She felt the weight of his question, as if it was a test. Would she still be in town? Was she looking at him for something potentially long-term?

"We'll see," she said in a teasing tone, knowing she'd still be here, and likely still pursuing what-ifs with this cowboy who was slipping into her life.

She hooked her arm through his and he guided her toward the bar, which stretched down the left side of the tavern. Three bartenders were working and a mass of occupied tables and chairs covered the uneven wood floor, with a small stage to the right. Toward the back a raised platform held pool tables, and the rear wall was covered with wood paneling and dartboards. Laura felt as though she had stepped onto a movie set, one where she wouldn't be surprised if people suddenly started breaking stools over each other's backs during a fight.

A bartender wearing a black cowboy hat took their order, and Levi rested an elbow on the bar, looking around the room. "No dancing tonight?"

"You want to dance, clear a spot," he replied.

Levi nodded as though taking the suggestion seriously.

"On your tab?" The bartender set down their drinks and Levi nodded again.

Laura looked out over the crowd and spotted Jackie. She was sitting with Jenny from Blue Tumbleweed, the two whispering together over what looked like margaritas. Jackie's expression turned curious as she spotted Laura, then Levi.

Laura felt her stomach drop. She sent Jackie a look of apology and lifted her shoulders, while mouthing, *"I'm sorry. Is this okay?"*

If her friend shook her head, Laura would be out of here. Immediately. No man was worth a friendship.

But Jackie broke into a beaming smile and gave a little jump in her chair, flashing Laura a thumbs-up while mouthing a giant *"Yes!".*

Laura let out a breath of relief.

"Come on," Levi said, oblivious to what had transpired behind his back. He picked up their drinks, steering Laura into the small space between the pool table platform and the tables of people listening to the band. Along the platform's railing was a narrow ledge, and Levi set the drinks down. He took her right hand in his left, his free hand going to her hip without hesitation as he swung her onto the narrow slice of dance floor.

The tempo of the song was upbeat and Laura let out a squeal as Levi moved with quick, precise motions she couldn't match, her feet landing on his more often than the floor beneath.

"Do you not know how to two-step?" Levi asked, slowing their pace.

Laura stumbled and shook her head. "Where would I two-step in New York?"

He tipped his head to look at their feet, and she leaned back so the brim of his hat didn't hit her in the forehead. He was just slightly taller in his boots and hat, and she loved that about him. That and his calm demeanor, patience and kindness.

"Slow, slow. Quick, quick," he said, his words matching his pace. She struggled, fearing she'd crash into someone's table.

"Can you let me lead?" he asked.

"Am I leading?"

"Yes."

"Well? Why can't I?"

"That's not how dancing works, Princess."

"Maybe it should," she retorted with a sassy jab of her chin. "You leading obviously isn't working."

He chuckled. "Maybe you should let the dancer lead."

"Maybe you should try teaching with words instead of just dragging me around the dance floor like a Neanderthal."

He laughed, but slowed his pace even more. "Wasn't ballet part of your princess lessons?"

"Quit calling me a princess," she said lightly. "And ballet was easy."

He laughed. "Ballet was easy? That's not what I've heard."

"Well, it was until I reached my first big growth spurt at age twelve and lost enough coordination that my instructor suggested I try something else."

"Ouch."

"Yeah."

Levi gave her hand a squeeze and picked up his pace again. "Quit thinking and follow my lead."

She closed her eyes, trying to feel the music. She crashed against his chest, opening her eyes to apologize.

He wiggled their joined hands. "Relax."

"Maybe if you stopped calling me a princess I would."

"You're thinking. You're trying. This is a cowboy dance, and we don't do either one of those things after a whiskey—and that's when we dance." They were moving again, her knees knocking his, her right foot landing on his left.

People at the tables had shifted, giving them more room to move on the makeshift dance floor.

"Quit looking at your feet," Levi prompted. "Look at me."

She did, then glanced away, feeling the power of his focus. She dared herself to look back, then to not look away. As she admired the flecks of gray in his blue eyes she felt the tension in her shoulders ease up, felt herself finding the rhythm as the next song slowed. The intimacy of holding eye contact kept her breathless and she struggled not to chicken out.

"There you go," Levi said, just loud enough for her to hear him.

The honest intensity in his eyes, along with the tenderness, was enough to spook her, but she stayed strong, forcing herself to keep her gaze locked on his, to delve into the depths she saw behind the open affection. Levi was the kind of man you could call in the middle of the night when your life had gone to crap, and he'd be there with a shovel and a smile.

"Thank you," she whispered.

"For what?"

She shrugged, unable to express the conviction that he would be there if she needed him, and how much that meant. They barely knew each other, but he was quickly becoming someone important to her. She lowered her cheek to his shoulder, moving close enough that she could match his movements without being jostled. She almost succeeded, and his hand moved from her waist to her lower back, his cheek coming to rest on her head. He was warm, strong, and everything a woman could depend upon without losing herself in the process. It was exhilarating and terrifying, and maybe exactly what she'd been looking for.

"We've started a trend," Laura said, lifting her head when the song ended, noting that several couples had joined them on the dance floor.

Levi smiled and took her hand, guiding her into a smooth twirl that reminded her of ballet more than country dancing.

"Time for a break?" he asked.

She nodded, reluctant to let him go. As they backtracked to where they'd left their drinks, someone snagged Levi, giving him a handshake and a slap on the back.

"Levi! I haven't seen you out on the floor since Janet left for college."

Levi's arm went around Laura's shoulders, pulling her close as his body stiffened. "It hasn't been that long."

"Yeah, but it hasn't been like this." The man smiled at Laura. "Name's Travis Nestner. Mayor of Sweetheart Creek."

"Pleased to meet you."

"Likewise. Welcome to town."

"Donna let you out of the house?" Levi teased. He said to Laura, "They have six-year-old triplets."

"Donna thinks I'm working." He lifted his beer with a smile.

"You are, aren't you?" Laura asked innocently. "You know, listening to the town's citizens about their daily concerns."

Travis grinned and gave a small lift of his cowboy hat. He said to Levi, "Hang on to this one."

"Plan to," he said, making Laura feel as though she was going to find herself married off before she had a say about it.

She slipped out from under his arm. "Easy there, cowboy. I'm not marrying you yet."

"Next week then?" There was a mischievous glint in his eyes that made her fight a smile. He'd definitely changed his perspective on her, it seemed.

"Tell her about Old Man Lovely and how he marries a couple each New Year's Eve," Travis suggested.

Levi waved off the comment. "It's a quirky Sweetheart Creek tradition," he explained to Laura.

He moved to retrieve their drinks from earlier, handing her hers. She shook her head.

"Is there something wrong with it?" he asked, before taking a long pull of his beer.

"It's not smart to leave your drink."

"It's not?" he asked, looking at his bottle.

"Someone could put something in it."

Levi slowly looked around. A few people called to him to compliment their dancing or to say hello as his gaze met theirs.

"Never mind," she muttered.

"Do you have to worry about drink tampering in the city?"

She really didn't want to think about New York and how cold

and foreign the social scene felt there. If that was her home, how could it feel so cold to her? How did this small town keep swallowing her heart every time she turned around?

"Who's Janet?"

"An ex."

"Broke your heart and it's never recovered?"

"Once bitten, twice shy is more like it."

"What did she do?" Laura froze for a second. "Wait! Betty's daughter, Janet Keys! The movie star?"

"Are you hungry?" he asked, a scowl forming a crease between his brows.

Wow. Janet was pure glamor and grace on the screen. It was hard to believe she'd lived in Sweetheart Creek and dated Levi the rancher. How had the two of them ever had anything in common? Then again, who was she to judge? She was a well-known model who was loving getting her boots dirty. Maybe Janet had a private side that was down-to-earth, too.

They ordered a plate of greasy appetizers, and while they waited for it to be ready they headed back onto the dance floor. She was getting the hang of it, Levi deftly altering his pace or movements to avoid most collisions. When the bartender waved to them they slid onto stools at the bar to enjoy their chicken wings and deep-fried pickles.

"Where did you learn to dance?" Laura asked.

Levi shrugged, his focus on the chicken wings.

"Lessons?"

He gave her a funny look.

"Aren't we trying to get to know each other better?" she asked sweetly.

Levi pushed away and swiveled to face her. His knees were touching hers, and she felt that familiar anticipation of not knowing what was going to happen next, but being confident that she would like it.

"There are regular barn dances where the community comes

together. Potluck. Either a local band plays or someone acts as DJ. People eat, dance and socialize until one or two in the morning. As a kid, you dance. You pick up moves, invent a few, or have people patiently run you through the steps." He shrugged as if it was nothing.

So far as she knew there wasn't anything similar to a barn dance in New York City. Maybe if you were a part of the Jewish community and attended bar mitzvahs and the like, you might have a multigenerational community coming together in a similar way. But for her family, the only dancing that ever happened was at a rare wedding, or if you took a class.

"It sounds fun," she said.

He nodded thoughtfully. "It is."

There was something about Levi and his life that made Laura long to be an integral part of it, if only to see how it felt. To be the one he looked for in a crowd, the one who made him smile and laugh.

She cast him a sidelong look, trying to sort out just how real her feelings were. That teenage crush was developing into more so fast she worried it was all just an illusion. And that was one thing she didn't want.

On the spot she decided she was going to hold off listing Luanne's house for sale. This was where she wanted to be. At least until she got to know Levi better.

When they'd polished off the chicken wings, Laura leaned forward, placing her hands on Levi's knees and focusing entirely on him. "Tell me more about Sweetheart Creek and all the other things you take for granted."

9

L evi had wanted to spend time with Laura on Sunday, like he had on Friday night and then Saturday, when they'd worked on training Target in her yard. But Sunday had been consumed by an issue with one of the herds, and he'd spent the day baking his hide out in the pastures during an unseasonably hot day, riding around on his ATV with Brant instead of spending it with Laura.

She'd been smart to suggest they get to know each other better, because the more he got to know her, the more he found to like. The problem was he wanted to discover everything about her immediately, and life, as usual, was intervening. But he'd see her for a little bit when she came in to work with the riders in a few hours.

He smiled as he sipped his Monday morning coffee from his usual spot, leaning against the backyard fence as the world woke up around him. Normally he'd be forming a strategic plan on how to tackle his day, but instead he found himself thinking about Laura and how she was no longer afraid to gaze into his eyes.

Whistling, he tipped his cup to allow the last drops to land in the grass, then headed to the house to drop it off so he didn't lose it while he went about his chores.

He crossed the stone patio to the kitchen's sliding door and tried to imagine what sort of birthday party Laura was planning to put on for him. As long as she was present, he was certain it would be a good one.

He'd kissed her goodbye late on Friday night, taking his time, her sweet lips on his, both of them wearing her lipstick when they were done. They'd done the same on Saturday, and he wondered if she'd be game for a kiss or two on the ranch or if "work" was off-limits.

As he opened the sliding door, singing filled his ears, the notes smooth and high. Definitely not one of his brothers. Laura was at the island, hunched over what looked like pie dough, singing. She looked up and gave him a smile so open and free that he lengthened his steps to reach her sooner. Just when he was about to slide his arms around her, his mother called out, "Good morning, Levi."

"What?" He stopped and turned.

She came bustling in, a box in her arms, and said to Laura, "I knew I had an extra punch bowl tucked away somewhere." She set it on the counter, then opened the oven door, sliding a tray inside with an efficiency that was wonderfully familiar.

"What's going on?" Levi asked.

"I'm learning to bake pies," Laura said, her voice tinkling with laughter as she swiped her doughy hands across the half apron hiding her curvy hips. She leaned forward, giving him a kiss on the lips.

He smiled and pulled her closer. "It looks like you're enjoying yourself."

"I am."

She was wearing a colorless lip gloss, and he guessed that she definitely planned on kissing him today, and not leaving a trace of their affection.

"I like the gloss," he whispered, kissing her again quickly.

"Laura can't put on this much food all by herself," his mother said, still bustling about the kitchen.

"You're serving lunch?" he asked, his interest piquing as he tried to figure out what the women were making.

"Yes. But I meant for the party," she stated. "Fifty people is a lot, you know."

"Fifty?" He hadn't invited that many.

"Fifty," his mom confirmed.

Laura had gone back to rolling out the ball of dough in front of her, and Levi stepped back so he wasn't in her way. He leaned in to kiss her again, and she obliged before shooing him off with a small smile. "You're distracting. We have lots to do before the riders come at ten."

The sun from last week had freckled her nose, and a healthy glow covered her cheeks, making her look even more gorgeous than ever. She was wearing the soft brown, square-toed cowboy boots he'd picked out for her on Saturday afternoon and had asked Jenny Oliver to deliver.

"Nice boots," he said.

"I have a footwear fairy."

He frowned, not partial to being called a fairy.

"How did you know my shoe size?" Laura asked.

"I'm the kind of man who notices things. Especially when someone's stepping on my toes while learning to dance."

He dodged the handful of flour she tossed at him.

His mother began nudging him toward the door. "Come on, now. I'm sure you have work to do. Quit distracting my help."

"I'm okay with frozen food," he said, sidestepping around his mom to slide in behind Laura, his arms going around her waist as he nuzzled her neck. "Just shove it all in the oven."

"Scurvy, trans fats and wasting away are not options," Maria retorted, using her I-mean-business tone.

Levi gave Laura a peck on the cheek, then began moving

toward the door before he got in trouble. He paused for a moment in the doorway to take in the sight of Laura working the dough, humming one of the songs they'd danced to on Friday. He'd been wrong about not having time for a girlfriend, and he could see how he'd been using the ranch as an excuse, a shield from putting himself out there, believing he'd never have anything close to this. The way Laura was weaving her way into his life was wonderful, and there was something about having her in his home, laughing and working with his mom, that made him feel strangely homesick for what could be.

He wanted this. He wanted this badly.

LAURA HAD BEEN HUMMING to herself all day. She and Maria had baked several fruit pies in the morning, among other items for the party, popping them into the freezer for Wednesday night. Working with Levi's mom had been like working with Levi, absorbing lots of information and always in motion. The woman had whizzed around the kitchen, rearranging things, making clucking noises whenever she found something put in the wrong place, or that hadn't been cleaned to her standards. Laura guessed she had been secretly pleased to see the boys had been faltering without her.

Having finished in the stables, Laura sauntered out into the afternoon sunshine. She inhaled the fresh air as her phone began to ring in her back pocket.

It was her sister.

"How's the house going?" Ava asked.

"Slowly, but that's okay. Did I tell you I'm fostering a puppy that chews just about everything in sight?" Target was currently at Brant's office for "day care" so she could get things done on the ranch without worrying about the pup.

"You always wanted a dog," her sister said. Ava's mom had

married Laura's dad when the girls were both fifteen, and while they'd lived under the same roof for only three years, they'd come to know each other as well as if they'd spent their entire childhoods together.

"True." Target was already worming his way into her heart and she wasn't sure what she'd do when Brant found him his forever family.

"How's the car?"

"Fixed!"

"No," Ava said in a disbelieving tone. She knew how many times Laura had taken the vehicle in to get its won't-start-when-hot issue fixed before finally giving up and living with it.

"I drove all over the place on Sunday and it started every time."

"Maybe it likes Texas."

"Maybe." Laura paused to reach down and pet an orange cat that was winding between her ankles. There was a lot to like about the Lone Star State.

"So what else is new out there?" her sister asked.

"I started a scholarship."

"You did?"

"Yup. And it's official. I've granted my first one already, and gave applications to several people in the community who I heard could benefit from the riding program. It feels good to give back to Sweetheart Creek. Everyone's so welcoming and kind."

"Wow! You don't move slowly, do you?"

She thought of Levi's words from the other day. "Some decisions you don't need to think about."

"Such as...?" Her sister's tone was a familiar one. Time to shift into dishing about men.

Laura smiled and ran her fingertips around the edge of her lips, checking for any wayward lipstick from their earlier kisses, before recalling she'd intentionally chosen a nude gloss so she and Levi could kiss to their hearts' content.

"I may have learned the two-step from a cowboy."

Ava laughed in amazement. "Does the poor man still have feet? Or are they black-and-blue and in casts?"

"I'm sure they're black-and-blue, but I barely stepped on him during the last song."

"More than one song? He sounds like a keeper."

Laura glanced toward the ranch house, the last place she'd seen Levi, even though he was likely out on the range now, being a cowboy. "He's wonderful."

"Is there a cowboy-related reason the house is going slowly?" her sister teased. "I know you wanted to spend a few weeks out there decompressing, but I'm starting to get the feeling you're not coming home soon."

Laura hesitated. She wasn't ready. Not by a long shot. Reina had managed to push her modeling gig for Emma Carrington back a few weeks, and Laura planned on savoring every moment before she had to take off for a while. "Where are you?"

"Taiwan," Ava replied, before her attention returned to what she wanted to know. "So really? Are you running away from home?"

"Wait…it must be the middle of the night there."

"Yeah, but I'm only here for a commercial." According to Ava, she barely needed half a functioning brain for location scouting when it came to commercials. "So, back to you. Should I be concerned? Because, for the record, I'm game with running away from home. You always talked about Texas like it was the best time of your life. I may harbor a bit of jealousy that our parents didn't meet sooner so I could have gone, too."

"You should come visit."

"You'll still be there when I get back? What about that perfume contract you were working on last Thursday when I called to gossip about the new hottie at work? Don't you have to go to New York?"

"Eventually. I have to fulfill a retainer contract, too. One last shoot."

"Don't drag your heels on the perfume deal."

"I'm not."

She was. She was dragging her heels on all of it. She liked being ensconced in nature and the small-town life. Going back to hammer out a contract felt like a step backward from the centered calm she'd found here over the past week. Maybe she *was* running away from home.

"I thought you wanted to be footloose and free by forty?" her sister asked.

"I do."

"Not working for minimum wage like me." Ava laughed, knowing full well she earned more than that. However, she joked that if you counted up all the hours she devoted to her job, the salary wasn't quite as impressive. "But seriously, Laura, don't let up now. You're so close to being exactly where you wanted to be at this stage of the game."

"Maybe I was playing the wrong game," she said.

Her sister was silent for a moment. "Are you okay?"

"Yeah, actually. Just…you know. Crossroads and reassessing things."

"Okay. You know you can call me anytime. Day or night."

"I do. Thanks. And vice versa."

"And Laura? Don't do anything too rash. A few contracts back in the city need only a few hours from you, so they can do their work in the background while you enjoy things there. It doesn't have to be one or the other. You have a good team that can take care of whatever it is you have on the go with your business, so you can still meet your goals."

Laura felt the old, unrelenting tug of the need to achieve more. More of this, more of that. Her mother had stressed that Laura do more with her life than she ever had—even though she'd gone back to college after the divorce. And her father? He'd echoed the sentiment, never letting Laura rest as her career rose and rose.

But Laura knew she'd earned enough. She was financially set, and she could comfortably retire as long as she didn't do anything too extreme spending-wise.

Still, the old feelings were hard to shake.

At the sound of a horse trotting her way, Laura walked around the end of the stable, to find Levi on top of a tall black stallion she had yet to meet.

"I have to go," she said.

"Hmm. Cowboy time?" Ava teased.

"Something like that."

"Have fun," her sister sang.

Laura ended the call and moved toward Levi, studying the dirty-looking white dog in his arms. As he came closer she realized it was a lamb, and that its mother was following along behind, Levi's dog making sure she stayed close.

Levi came alongside Laura, tipping his head toward a large, empty pen beside the red barn. Long grass obscured some of the metal mesh fencing. "Can you open the gate for me?"

"What have you got there?" she asked, hurrying to lift the latch.

"A struggling lamb."

Lupe immediately rounded up the ewe and another lamb Laura hadn't noticed earlier.

"How strong are you?" Levi asked, sizing her up. His horse had stopped outside the pen, shifting from foot to foot.

She studied the lamb doubtfully. It was adorable, but she wasn't sure she could handle the squirming animal, and especially safely transfer it from Levi's arms to her own with him still up on his horse. "How heavy is it?"

"Fairly. Here, hold the reins."

She did, and with a core strength she had underestimated, Levi lifted himself in one stirrup, then slid off the tall stallion, the lamb still clasped in his arms. Landing with knees bent, he paused to catch his balance for a moment, then set the lamb on its feet inside the pen. It hurried to its mother's side with a plaintive bleat.

Levi gave Lupe some hand signals and the dog guarded the gate as Levi began to close it, the two of them slipping out at the last moment.

Lupe, now off duty, came to Laura, smiling and waiting to be petted. She stroked his dusty fur, then followed Levi who took the reins back for his horse. They headed toward what she thought of as the working stable, a building she hadn't yet been inside, and was set farther away from the house than the riding arena.

"I didn't know you had sheep."

"They're Ryan's. He said something about getting some that sounded smart, I fell for it, and now I have sheep."

"They're yours?"

"Well, he doesn't do anything to help with them, and I raised my hand at the auction last month with the winning bid. So, yeah. I guess they're mine."

Levi looked disgruntled, but Laura knew it was mostly an act.

"How do you know this lamb is struggling?" she asked.

"Its twin is bigger, thriving. I think the smaller one isn't getting enough milk."

"What will you do? Make them take turns or something?" She fell into step beside him, and he leaned close enough to give her a quick kiss.

"No, we'll bottle-feed to get it caught up. My guess is that the mom either can't produce enough milk or its sibling is bullying it away from the teat any time it tries to feed."

"Poor thing."

In the stable, Levi took the saddle, blanket, bridle and reins off his horse and released it into a separate pasture from the kids' horses.

This building was darker than the riding barn, the ceilings lower, and with a wood planked floor. Laura followed Levi into a storage room near the main door. Inside were various bottles and containers, and it smelled a bit like a veterinarian office. Levi grabbed a container of powder and a large baby bottle, then mixed up some formula in the sink before turning to Laura. "Ever fed a lamb?"

She shook her head, smiling. "Can I?"

He grinned and handed her the large bottle. "Come on, let's go earn those cowboy boots."

"It's not enough to just look good in them?"

They headed back to the pen, where the momma sheep and her lambs gave them leery looks with their large dark eyes. The ewe stepped forward, the lambs falling in behind her woolly body.

"The first time you bottle-feed is the trickiest," Levi said. "But once this little guy figures out we have food he won't be so nervous next time."

Levi whistled and Lupe came to his side. Levi let the dog into the pen and gave some hand signals. The dog quickly cornered the weaker lamb, herding it toward Levi, who had opened the gate to a separate smaller pen. Once inside, he deftly and gently pinned the small animal against the mesh, squeezing the bottle's nipple to send droplets onto the end of its nose. When he released the lamb it backed away, toward where its mother was calling to it through the metal gate that separated them. The lamb licked its nose, and gave Levi a curious look. Levi squatted, holding out the bottle.

Laura watched as he got the lamb used to him and feeding from the bottle before quietly calling her over. She crouched beside him and he helped her position the nipple for the little one to feed. Almost at once the lamb gave a surprisingly strong tug, pulling the bottle from her grip. Levi had been at the ready and caught it, repositioning it back in her hands.

"He's strong," she said in wonder.

"And hungry."

As the lamb emptied the bottle, its huge, dark eyes barely leaving her, Laura felt a tugging in her heart. This was amazing. Everything she did here felt so real, so alive. She was right in the midst of it, not like anything she did in her modeling career.

When Levi finally released the lamb back into the bigger pen, Laura took in her surroundings—the green trees circling the area, the rustle of leaves in the wind, Levi, the animals... With a pang, she realized she truly didn't want to go back to New York. She'd been away for only a short time, and yet she could no longer make New York feel real. Her bed, her couch, the familiar, well-trod route to her agent's office... It no longer felt like home. It was just a place. A time in her life that had brought her to this moment, to this version of herself.

Levi was watching her with a look of tenderness in his eyes. As he opened his mouth to speak, she quickly blurted, "I guess we'd better go wash this out."

She waved the bottle, and with long strides hurried back into the stable, trying to outrun the realization that this place and the man behind her meant a whole lot more to her than she was prepared for.

ON TUESDAY after supper Levi led two saddled horses toward the back door of the ranch house, sending the kittens that had been playing on the patio in all directions. He knocked on the kitchen's glass sliding door and Laura looked up from where she was at the counter, decorating cookies.

She opened the door in concern, Target darting around her feet in excitement at Levi's arrival. "What's wrong?"

"I thought maybe you'd like to go for a sunset ride."

"The party's tomorrow. There's still lots to do. We kind of got roped into making cookies for a fundraiser at the elementary school, too." She looked over her shoulder at Maria, who gave a little wave of her fingers.

"I can handle the rest of this. Go enjoy the evening, Laura. Target can stay in here with me."

Levi gave his mom a grateful smile and took Laura by the hand, leading her outside and passing her Clover's reins.

"I guess it's a good thing I'm wearing my new boots," she mused.

"A true cowgirl never takes them off."

"Not even for sleep? And anyway, I haven't fully earned these boots yet."

He disagreed, but knew not to argue. They mounted the horses and rode slowly past the barn and stables, before moving into a canter when they reached a trail across flat, open grasslands that led to the creek.

"This is the life," Laura said, as their horses trotted through a grove of oaks and shrubs. "It's so quiet and peaceful."

"Fresh air and hot cowboys," Levi said, tipping his hat brim. "At your service."

Laura laughed so hard he worried she was going to accidentally spur the horse or fall off.

"You know I do still have some business to attend to in New York. I'm not a full-grown Texas cowgirl. Not yet."

Yet. Such a loaded, sweet word.

"I know." He also knew the ranch was growing on her, and that she seemed more and more relaxed and at ease around the animals. He'd also noted how she tensed up whenever she talked about the city, contracts and her old life.

They rode on for a while, taking cow trails at times, opening gates here and there as they moved through different pastures. He kept an eye out for fences in need of work as they went, but mostly kept his focus on Laura and how content and radiant she seemed up on Clover.

"You're a good rider," he commented. She'd obviously spent more time on horseback than he'd realized.

"I don't know which human civilization first decided that riding horses was a good idea, but I'm glad they did."

"Life would be a lot different for me if they hadn't." He pointed to a gate blocking their way. "You want to open this one?"

"Sure." She slid off the horse and went to the barbed-wire fence. Hugging the main post like he'd done, she pulled the wire gate with its wooden supports toward her so she could lift the loop of wire that latched it to the fence, then dragged the loose gate to the side so Levi could ride through, leading her horse.

"Make sure you get it closed properly. Otherwise the cattle rub against it, knock it down and escape."

"Got it." She struggled a minute, but eventually got the floppy gate upright and secured.

They went down the slope toward Sweetheart Creek, which ran through the ranch and then on to the town, giving the community its name.

"This is Sweetheart Creek and my waterfall," he said, pointing to some faster moving water to his left.

"That's not a waterfall, is it?" she said doubtfully.

"Not at the moment maybe. But when we get flash floods, this outcropping steers part of the flow that way and it shoots down over those rocks." He waved his hand. "There are a couple of places along here where veritable rapids occur after a heavy rain, so my brothers and I each claimed a waterfall."

"You spent a lot of time out here as kids?" Laura asked.

He nodded.

"It must've been an amazing place to grow up."

"It was. Still is." He glanced over his shoulder at the creek, which looked languid and innocent this dry autumn evening, but Levi knew from experience how quickly it could become a danger during floods. He'd done some growing up here when he was fifteen after he'd stormed off when his four younger brothers had refused to listen to his advice about the flooding creek. He'd left them there, and they'd all come close to losing Ryan that day. Levi supposed that no matter where a person spent their childhood there would be times like that. You grew into the space you were born in, pushing the boundaries and finding the dangers no matter how innocent or obvious they might seem.

"Do you want a family?" he asked Laura, shaking off the past. He understood she'd had a big career, and had maybe decided she didn't want kids. He knew he did, though. Lots of them. But she might consider herself past the age where she might want two or three, or even any at all.

Laura was quiet for a long moment, then finally said, "I do." She turned to take in his reaction. He was careful to simply accept it, to not say anything.

"We missed the sunset," he remarked instead, noting that the sun had dipped below the horizon, the sky streaked with pinks and oranges.

They turned the horses back toward the ranch house, hearing cattle calling to each other in the distance. As they rode Laura asked, her tone tentative, "Do you? Want kids, that is?"

"I practically have them already named."

She turned in the saddle, relaxing as she took a better look at him. "Why am I not surprised?"

"What? The other men you've dated haven't wanted kids?"

"I didn't want to assume."

There was something about her body language that told him to tread carefully and not move too fast or he might scare her off. "I'm not in a big hurry yet. I have a lot of changes envisioned for the ranch, and implementing them will keep me busy. But one day." Soon. Very soon, hopefully.

That cloud in Laura's eyes was returning again—the one he knew masked pain and hurt. She bit her bottom lip, looking more perturbed by his statement than he'd expected her to. They rode in silence as he tried to think of a way to delve into the reasoning behind her reaction. He'd thought they were both in step on the path to their hearts' desire of love, family, happiness.

Before he realized it, they'd crested the small rise before the last fence between them and the yard.

"I'll get the gate," Laura said, when they spotted Levi's great-uncle leaning against the fence post, waiting.

"Nice romantic ride?" Henry asked. "Forgot you were gonna bring me that stallion for breeding, did you? Don't worry, your mom got him loaded into the trailer for me while y'all were out gallivanting."

Levi had forgotten. But who could blame him? When it came to spending time with his dour relative or Laura, she would always eclipse him.

10

As promised, Levi left the pastures early on his birthday, showered and was ready to play his role as the guest of honor at his party. With his hair still damp, as well as still in need of a cut, he trotted into the kitchen looking for Laura, who had been working all afternoon with his mom, getting things ready.

Through the patio door he saw her sitting in one of the lawn chairs, tossing a ball for Target to fetch. She was laughing, watching the puppy overshoot the ball more often than not, skid to a stop, then come tearing back, the ball in his mouth.

His mom came into the kitchen, carrying a tray. "Do you know how long it took me to find this?" she asked. "You boys managed to rearrange everything while I was gone." Maria followed his gaze. "She's lovely, isn't she?"

"She is."

"When's she heading back to New York?"

"We're giving ourselves some time to see where things take us. She's waiting to put Luanne's place up for sale."

His mom smiled. "I like the sound of that. But I thought she had a photo shoot to take care of."

"She's retired."

"She said something about a retainer contract. It sounded as though it was coming up soon."

"First I've heard she's still under contract." An unwelcome feeling of dread settled over Levi.

As though sensing they were talking about her, Laura turned in her chair, brightening when she spotted him through the glass. Levi opened the door, stepping out into the day's dwindling heat. "Howdy, Princess."

She rolled her eyes at the nickname. "I think mucking out the stables this morning proved I'm not a princess."

He chuckled, pulling her to her feet so he could wrap his arms around her and give her a gentle kiss that soon turned deeper. He could kiss this woman forever.

Around them the patio was decorated with balloons and streamers, and little lights strung up for when the sun set.

"It looks great out here."

Laura perked up. "Do you like it?"

He slid an arm around her shoulders, pulling her in for another kiss as he said, "Love it."

She made a contented sound and kissed him back, her fingers tugging on the longish hair at the nape of his neck.

Target was popping up on his hind legs, bouncing off Laura's thigh.

"Fun trick," Levi said.

"Unless he's been digging in the backyard. Then he makes me muddy. He has some destructive tendencies."

"You can give him back to Brant."

She lifted the puppy into her arms for a snuggle. "I could. Or I could train him not to eat my high heels. You know he never chews my cowboy boots."

As far as he could figure, she had a growing collection for the amount of time she'd spent in Texas. "I guess the dog is a true Texan. I heard he learned about horses yesterday?"

She looked chagrined. "I shouldn't have brought him into the stable."

Levi nodded. "We all learn a few lessons the hard way. You can train him out of most of this stuff. He's a smart dog."

"You'd warned me about taking him in there, though. I had him on his leash, but he slipped out of his collar."

"It happens, and before you blame yourself or start talking about not earning your boots, let me tell you you're great with the things that matter." He ruffled the fur on Target's back, noting that Laura had switched him from a collar to a harness. "This little guy will get used to the simple life, and learn it's not so simple." He winked. "And that horses don't like being nipped at by busy little pups."

"Your uncle Henry is really upset about the scholarship."

"Henry?" Levi paused in surprise. "How does he know?"

She shrugged. "He's claiming I'm throwing my money around and trying to get people to like me."

"People liked you before they knew you were behind the scholarship."

She didn't look as though she believed it.

"He's not someone you should listen to."

"It makes me wonder, though."

"Wonder what?"

She was silent for a moment. "Just… I guess that maybe… I know I don't fit in. I'm different, and my career—"

"You're the same where it matters. You care about this community and its people. You're kind, and you'll always have a home here."

Her expression softened, but there was something in her gaze he couldn't quite figure out. And that sent a trickle of worry down his spine.

As Levi introduced Laura to his guests under the twinkling lights she'd strung above the patio, Laura carefully held Target's leash so he wouldn't get into trouble.

"Laura, I heard you're helping out in the riding stable?" Levi's cousin Nick Wylder asked, catching her attention. He had grown up on the ranch, but now worked on a nearby one called Blueberry Creek II, owned by Alexa McTavish, who Laura had met earlier. The woman had come to Texas by way of Montana and South Carolina, in what had to amount to a good story.

"Laura's a natural," Levi said, sliding an arm across her shoulders.

"So I've heard." Nick seemed to have that same way of assessing her as the other Wylders.

"She's great with ailing lambs, too," Levi added, as Myles joined them, beer in hand.

Laura kept her mouth shut. Only that morning the ewe had nearly rammed her when she'd tried to cull the little one out of the pen for its bottle-feeding. Levi had made it look easier than it was. Thankfully, Lupe had been nearby and had come running when she'd yelped in fear.

"Levi keeps talking about hiring someone to help out around here. We should hire you full-time," Myles said, taking a swig of his drink while watching her. He made a sour face. "How do I keep pulling out bottles of that disgusting Lambic stuff of Ryan's?" He looked over his shoulder, scowling at his younger brother, who was laughing with April MacFarlane. Ryan grinned and toasted Myles with a bottle of store-bought beer.

"I'm pretty sure I'm not qualified," Laura said, though she appreciated Myles's kind words.

"Y'all still haven't replaced me?" Nick asked, a hint of incredulity in his tone. "I've been gone since June!"

Levi shrugged and sighed.

"Ryan's being a tightwad and keeps refusing to approve the expenditure," Myles stated.

Levi pulled Laura closer, giving her a kiss on the cheek. "Good thing I found my cowgirl."

"Wait. I thought you were too busy for a girlfriend?" Nick's eyes narrowed as if he was preparing to give Levi a difficult time.

"I thought wrong." He smiled at Laura.

"Hey, want a beer?" Nick asked her, reaching into one of the mini horse troughs Maria had hauled onto the deck, then filled with ice and bottled drinks.

"I don't like beer, thanks," Laura replied.

"So, you're not a real cowgirl despite what Levi claims?" Nick's eyes were dancing.

She raised her hands in defeat. "You got me! I'm a complete fake. I still like girlie things."

"I'll mix you a Cosmo," Myles offered, eyebrows raised in question.

"Thanks. That would be nice."

"Want an umbrella in it?" Nick teased.

"Of course! My motto is go girly, or go home."

"So you're half in New York and half here?" Nick asked.

Levi was holding his beer bottle, frowning at the label.

"For now, sort of." She was having fun playing cowgirl, but knew she couldn't put real life on hold forever. Her sister was right in saying that Laura needed to make sure she still had projects working in the background to get her where she wanted to be for her retirement. Because if she didn't settle down here, she needed a plan B.

But it was tough. This was where she wanted to be, and how was she going to split her time between the city and the ranch? How would Levi take it when she told him she had to leave for a few weeks, when his life was so obviously focused here? And if she wasn't a full-time cowgirl would she still fit into his life? Leaving even for a week or two was going to be difficult for both of them.

She caught Levi watching her with a look that made her want

to launch herself into his arms and never let go. Why did being with him feel so right, when it was so unexpected? Why did it make her want to throw away everything she'd spent the last fifteen years working toward?

Laura's phone rang and she pulled it from her pocket, gratefully excusing herself from the group and Levi's probing gaze. Plugging her free ear with a finger, she stepped to the edge of the patio as she answered, then moved past a cluster of partygoers gathered by a beautiful rose trellis on the lawn before stopping by a swing set under the trees. Behind her bursts of laughter broke the quiet of the night.

"I have another offer on your aunt's house."

"I don't even have it listed!" Laura frowned and hooked Target's leash over the swing's armrest, staring at the fallow vegetable garden. Would she still be here to help lay out rows next spring?

"I know, but this offer is a legitimate one, from the same people as before. They really want this house, and you might not get another offer in a long time. The market is pretty depressed in this area. They're willing to match your to-be list price, with a gentle request for possession in two weeks—that's mid-October."

The young family. They needed a home, didn't they? And she was holding on to a property that she would be coming and going from over the next few months as she settled contracts in the city. They needed it more than she did, as she could easily rent a simple place in town that suited her needs.

Laura scanned the crowd on the patio, looking for Levi. He was standing near the grill, facing her, his cowboy hat shadowing his eyes. Behind him was his uncle Henry, frowning in her direction, with someone vaguely familiar standing beside him, camera slung around his neck.

Laura sent Henry a determined look. She wasn't done in Sweetheart Creek. Not yet.

But she also knew she had to accept the offer. If she didn't sell now, she might not be able to find a buyer when she wanted one.

"Start the paperwork. That house is now sold."

SOMETHING WAS UP. Levi stood by the barbecue, afraid to move toward Laura. Something had shifted for her. He'd felt her withdraw during their conversation with his brother and cousin, and now, seeing her expression after the phone call, he knew something had happened.

She had her chin tipped up, and the smile she flashed as she approached him was as stiff as Carmichael before a rainstorm.

"Go talk to her," his mom said, nudging him with her elbow. She looked worried, too.

"Yeah," he said, his gaze drifting back to Laura.

Maria had been cooking meals on the ranch for the past few days, and like a tap, all complaints from Carmichael and his brothers had been instantly shut off. Every night there was a full table, just like old times, and once even Laura had joined them. It was exactly what he'd been afraid to wish for. And now...now he worried that it wasn't going to last.

"Go," his mother urged.

He nodded, moving toward Laura.

Henry and a man with a camera stopped him.

"Happy birthday, Levi," said the stranger. "Can I ask you a few questions about the new scholarship your girlfriend started here on the ranch?"

"I'm sorry, who are you?" And how did everyone suddenly know about Laura's role in it? He'd cautioned her to be careful about going public with the funding details.

"I'm a reporter with—"

His father caught Levi by the arm, pulling him away from them. "Sorry, guys! I need to say hello to my birthday boy." He said it a bit too loudly, while Sophia, standing next to him, smiled, no doubt feeling awkward being on her husband's ex-wife's turf.

Levi apologized over his shoulder to the reporter, pleased at least that Henry seemed to be coming round about the scholarships and Laura's help, even if it was going public. He turned to his dad and stepmom. "Sorry, I've been neglecting you. Did you find food?" He glanced toward the food table, where Carmichael had pulled up a chair near Maria's seven-layer dip and was quite happily making his way through it.

"We did."

"We bought you a new hat," Sophia said, over the sound of cattle calling to each other from the closest pasture. "Jenny said you'd been admiring it in her store. I hope you hadn't already picked one up for yourself."

He shook his head. "I haven't, thanks."

"It's on the table over there," his dad said. "I know you said no gifts, but we couldn't help it. I was going to head inside and leave it in your room, but I didn't want to overstep, here on your ranch."

"Your name is still on the deed."

"You know, my lawyer's been calling me every week. He doesn't like having my name still on everything. Liability and what-not."

"Yeah, and I don't like you nagging me over it." Levi felt his patience snap. "Try nagging your other four sons. I know what claim I want to make when it comes to this place."

Levi caught sight of Brant's round, worried eyes across the patio, and he lowered his voice. "I've been keeping this ranch running, Dad. I've jumped in with both feet. I'm paying the bills and keeping the place afloat, as well as ensuring your retirement fund remains at a sufficient level."

Sophia looked upset with the conversation, but Roy just hooked his thumbs in his belt loops and leaned back on his heels.

"I need my name off the deed and any remaining contracts. Don't let things go south on me, boy. It's not just you you're looking out for."

"Yeah, I get it. Trust me." He was responsible for the whole Wylder crew. From the youngest, Ryan, on up to Carmichael. He'd failed once, not taking his responsibilities as the eldest of the boys seriously and had bucked his orders. As a consequence, he almost lost Ryan downstream. He would have if Brant hadn't gone for help, Cole hadn't kept his eye on where Ryan was, and Myles hadn't risked his own life by jumping in after Ryan. Levi didn't plan to loosen his grip on the ranch and its needs, nor forget what was needed of him, because this time he didn't have all four brothers there to cover for him if he messed up.

"I heard about the riding program," his dad said quietly, concern evident in his tone. "Henry said you brought in a fashion model to replace Betty."

"My girlfriend. She's doing well with it."

Sophia smiled. "That's wonderful. Mrs. Fisher told me what she did for Donnie."

"The riding program is an important part of this ranch," Roy said. As though the nearby cattle agreed, they let out a loud call. Why did they sound so close tonight?

"It is," Uncle Henry said, joining them. "It's important. What I want to know is what that Laura woman knows about ranch life. She's a city gal, not a cowgirl."

"That shouldn't matter if she's getting the job done," Sophia said, her spine straightening.

"I have everything covered," Levi said. "Trust me."

LAURA SLIPPED her phone into her back pocket and wondered how she was going to tell Levi that she had to be out of her aunt's house in two weeks. And she had to leave Texas, too. He was going to think she was getting cold feet and running off on him. But Sweetheart Creek had become home, and her heart was here with Levi. Surely he understood that.

She was crossing the yard to join him when she felt the ground start to tremble. Earthquake? Then she heard a thundering that she couldn't quite place. As she searched the crowd for Levi, cowboy hats pivoted in her direction. Toward the stables. Toward the pastures behind her.

Lupe started barking and flew off his spot on the patio, instantly heading toward the sound. Men separated themselves from the crowd, advancing with a hurried authority. Laura backed toward the patio as several tons of frightened cattle came ripping down the oak-lined path from the stables, a brown-and-white blur headed directly toward the patio. Lupe was nipping at legs, barking and yipping, trying to gain control of the herd. Laura screamed, afraid the dog would get trampled.

Maria grabbed her arm in a tight grip, hauling her toward the house. "Hurry!"

"What about Lupe?"

"He knows what he's doing."

"Target! Where's Target?"

"Get inside. It's not safe out here."

"Well," Henry drawled, as he hurried past them toward where the vehicles were parked. "That's about a hundred panicked animals ready to destroy everything in their path. Good luck to you all."

"You get out there and help!" Maria shouted at him, while shoving Laura into the house. She closed the patio door behind them and several other guests, waving her arms to ensure the herd didn't move in their direction as they tore into the backyard. The rose trellis suddenly buckled, then disappeared.

"Good!" she muttered. "I needed an excuse to get rid of those. Ruth planted them in an awkward spot and Carmichael would never let me move them."

Laura stared, horrified. The herd was spreading out, trampling everything in the wide chute the backyard created for them, funneling them around the house.

A flash of color flew through the sky as the herd rammed the buffet table, sending bowls and platters into the air.

"The food!"

"Leave it." Maria left Laura's side, calling, "Keep waving your arms so they don't come through the window, thinking it's a way to escape. I'll be back. Stay inside until you're sure they're gone for good. April, you stay with her." April, her son at her side, joined Laura at the patio door while other guests followed Maria and her various other instructions.

Laura heard the front door shut.

She stayed at the patio door, instinctively stepping back when the big animals came too close before remembering to continue waving. The herd ripped across the patio, knocking over chairs, tables, planters, destroying everything in their wake. Behind them she saw a small flash of brown and black.

"Target!" His leash was trailing behind him and he was happily tearing back and forth after frightened cattle, barking and sending them into a frenzy.

"No," April said calmly, placing a hand on Laura's arm as though expecting to have to hold her back.

Laura covered her mouth with her hands, helplessly eyeing the destruction as the herd disappeared around the side of the house, her dog still in pursuit.

Men were already on horseback, letting out sounds she'd heard only in movies, as they worked to get the herd under control.

Laura ran to the front of the house, watching from the living room window along with Sophia and Jenny as the stream of cattle ripped up the lawn, taking out small shrubs and setting off a car alarm before blundering out onto the road. Laura groaned when she saw them jostle her little VW Beetle out of the way as though it barely weighed a thing.

When they finally disappeared, the silence was almost eerie, the air filled with dust. Laura stepped out onto the porch.

"I'll bet you that gate by the back stable wasn't closed properly last night," Henry announced from the front step. "Hope your little sunset ride with Levi was worth the cost you just incurred him and the ranch."

Laura felt her heart drop.

"Levi keeps telling us that the two of you have things handled out here and that we should trust him." Henry sized her up. "I'm not so sure he hasn't been blinded."

"There is nothing to be blinded by," Laura said, finding her voice. "I'm helping out."

"By throwing your money around or by letting out a few thousand grand worth of cattle?"

"I did not throw my money around," she stated, her voice shaking. "I am supporting this community as well as this ranch's riding program."

"Well, just hope nobody gets hurt and the damage isn't too bad with this little fiasco," Henry said, moving toward his truck. He paused, giving her a knowing half smile. "Say, whose little dog was that riding the herd, anyway?"

11

When the cattle had been rounded up, the horses put back out to pasture, the men all thanked for stepping in, and his father argued with over how he was running the ranch, Levi sought out Laura.

As he came to the back of the house, Target nestled in the crook of his arm, the scene shocked him. The patio was in ruins, broken tables and chairs stacked at the edge, along with bags of trash. Bits of food still splattered the stones and the house's siding despite the cleanup. The barbecue was dented, the patio's carefully laid pieces broken and upended in places. It looked like a stampede had been through, all right.

"Did you see Laura's car?" Levi's mother asked, coming up alongside him. She'd taken the truck and helped head off the herd by circling out on back roads to meet them face-to-face. She must have broken some speed records on those gravel roads tonight, and her help had been invaluable.

"No, I didn't," Levi replied, absently petting Laura's tired dog.

"The front wheel well doesn't look too good. How is she handling things? Henry said the gate was her fault."

"I haven't spoken to her yet, but the gate could have been

anyone's." Although Hank had said he hadn't been through it since moving the herd, making Laura the last one to secure the gate. It was clear it had swung open, the cattle deciding to mosey through, and then the little dog in his arms had come along to have some fun.

Levi and his mom moved to the patio door and he could see Laura working at the sink, elbow deep in soapy dishwater.

"She reminds me a lot of Janet," Maria murmured. "She's bigger than this town."

"She likes it here," he said, aware that he was sounding defensive.

"I know. That's not what I meant."

Levi frowned at his mother. Laura was different than Janet. Janet had always been running toward glamor, whereas Laura seemed happy to leave it behind. She was running to the ranch, not away from it.

He said good-night to his mom who was heading back to her own place, and slid the patio door open. He came up behind Laura and brushed a kiss against her cheek. Her eyes slowly closed, as though she was committing the kiss to memory.

Target wiggled in his grasp, climbing up Laura's shoulder to lick her cheek. Tears filled her eyes as she turned to them, taking the dog in her arms.

"Is everyone okay?" she asked.

"I think so."

"I am so sorry, Levi. I thought I had his leash secured." She set Target down on the floor. "And I thought I fastened the gate right, too."

"Yeah, things got exciting, didn't they?"

"I ruined your party and the patio. Your furniture. The lawn. Landscaping. Cars!" She was teary with remorse. "I'm so sorry."

"Shh." Levi placed a kiss on her lips, sliding his arms around her waist. "And I'm the one sorry about your car. My ranch should be a safe place for you both." He lightened his tone. "But hey, I rented the new Ford Mustang last June and they're pretty nice if you're looking for a fun car."

She buried her head against his shoulder.

"I should turn thirty-five more often," he murmured, savoring the way she felt in his arms.

She lifted her head to give him an incredulous look.

"That was likely the most memorable birthday of my life."

"And all my fault. Did anything off the property get wrecked? I'll replace everything that got broken in the stampede."

"They went down the road, so no. We lucked out." He looked down at Target, stretched out on the cool floor and half asleep. "You have quite the little herding animal there."

A deep line formed between her brows. "Where's Lupe?"

"With Brant."

"Oh."

"Is there still cake?"

She looked upset again, and Levi started laughing. "Don't tell me the stampede took it out?"

"They took out everything," she said, her voice edging on hysteria. "Wait, why is Lupe with Brant?"

Levi inhaled, wishing she hadn't asked that. "He hurt his leg."

"No," she said on an exhale.

"He's okay. Brant's just taking him for an X-ray."

"You should be with him."

"I wanted to check in on you."

"I'm okay."

"And Laura?" He waited until she looked up. "These things happen."

"No, they don't."

"They do. And before you start saying you're not a real cowgirl, they make mistakes, too."

She exhaled again and rubbed an eye, looking morose.

"Hey, come here." He pulled her into his arms again. "Where's your smile?"

She looked even more upset. "I got an offer on the house."

"Another one? But I thought it wasn't even listed." He stiffened, holding her away so he could see her better.

"It's from the same family," Laura said, "and it's a good offer."

"The family?" When he found Brant he was going to lock him in the root cellar.

She ran her hands down her short denim skirt, and when she wouldn't meet his eye, a bad feeling crept in.

"I took it."

She was leaving.

"When's possession?" he asked, trying to rein himself in. If Laura had a few months before then they could continue dating, and she could simply move into the ranch house when it was time for her to leave her aunt's. He knew it was quick, but he also knew what he wanted: Laura. It was that simple. That easy. He could no longer imagine not having her in his life.

"Two weeks."

Levi adjusted his hat with a jerk, trying to hide the fact that the news felt like a punch to the gut.

She reached for his waist, as if she might slide her arm around him. "I have business that needs wrapping up in New York, anyway."

"I thought you retired."

"I still have a brand. A name. An agent. New contracts to iron out and old contracts to complete. I have opportunities to exploit."

Exploit. What was she talking about?

She sighed. "And even though I retired I still have obligations with a company that had me on retainer. If I don't go on this upcoming shoot I'll be in breach of contract. It's not worth the kill fee."

"You're going back to modeling? I thought you were happy here."

"I am. But I also need to do these things. If I go back and take care of this stuff, then I can be retired for real by age forty. I won't have to worry about money ever again."

Money? There was so much more to life than money.

"I thought you wanted to start a family, and live a simple life where you can breathe the air?" He could barely think over the buzzing in his ears. She was leaving. She wasn't retired. She still had one foot firmly placed in her world of glitz and glamor.

"I do."

There was only one thing he needed to know, and he had a feeling her answer would be a lie meant to cushion the blow to his heart.

"Are you coming back?"

***

LAURA FOUGHT BACK the tears as she walked across the yard to her car. She'd had a feeling Levi would make the worst out of her having to leave in order to keep up with her life. She'd assured him she was coming back, but the look in his eyes told her he didn't believe her, and that she'd just put a giant wedge between them, like she'd feared she might.

She had also thought she could handle ranch life. But two moments of not paying attention, with Target and the pasture gate, and she had created a near disaster that had injured Levi's dog, destroyed his yard and birthday party, and could have seriously hurt someone.

She was lucky it hadn't been worse.

What had really hurt, though, was how Levi had assumed she had been dishonest with him and didn't want a family. It had felt as though he'd questioned every moment they'd shared over the past week and a half. She hadn't expected it, and after the worry and torment over the stampede disaster, her heart felt tender.

She stopped beside her car. The cattle had pushed it aside as if it was made of cardboard, and she hoped it had suffered only a few minor dents, giving it character. It hadn't. The driver-side front wheel was sloped inward as though the axle had buckled, making the car undrivable.

She sniffed and tried to pull herself together, but the loss of her Beetle was the last straw.

"Need a ride?" The quiet drawl behind her was characteristically Carmichael.

Laura wiped her eyes and turned.

"Sorry about your party," he said.

"No, I'm sorry." She sniffed again. "I ruined so much."

"I have a feeling it was that furry bastard in your arms," Carmichael said, gesturing at Target. He tipped his head toward one of the trucks parked in the yard. "Let's give you a ride home, shall we?"

She thought of what Maria had said about the roses Carmichael's wife had planted.

"I'm sorry about the trellis. I'll rebuild it and replace the rosebushes."

Carmichael was quiet for a long moment, then said, "Maria never did like them there. I suppose it's between you and her where they go next. If you even want roses."

Laura wasn't sure what to say, so didn't reply as she climbed into the truck with Target. He immediately walked across the seat to sniff Carmichael.

"You smell my dog, Missy?" he asked, his voice lifting as he spoke to the dog. "You'll probably never meet her. She's a pretty little thing not meant for ranch life." He tousled Target's ears and the dog sat down beside him and stared forward, even though he was too small to see over the dashboard.

"I fear I was digging in about the roses just for the sake of digging in," Carmichael said, starting the engine.

Laura nodded, and remained silent for the rest of the drive, knowing Carmichael wouldn't mind. He stopped in front of her house and pulled a candy bar from the breast pocket of his shirt.

After unpeeling the wrapper, he broke it in two and handed her half.

Target leaped up, trying to take it.

Carmichael tipped his hand away from the dog and clicked his tongue. The dog sat.

"Chocolate's not good for dogs. But it's good for a woman who's had a hard day." He offered Laura half again, and the dog stayed where he was.

"Thank you," she said, and sat with him in a comfortable silence while they savored the sweet chocolate.

"You know..."

Carmichael didn't finish the sentence, so she finally asked, "Know what?"

"I was going to say it was just a car, but it seems like it's more than that to you."

"I bought it with my very first paycheck from modeling. It's a symbol of my independence, I guess." Something she'd achieved a long time ago and probably didn't need a symbol for any longer.

"I guess now it's a symbol of change."

"The end of an era."

"I was also going to say that I overheard Levi talking about your future plans there in the kitchen. It's been a long time since he opened his heart to a woman, and you're good for him. You remind him that there's more to life than working on that ranch and making sure I have enough money in my bank account. I appreciate his dedication, but it's been good seeing him smile."

"Are you telling me not to give up on him?" She cast Carmichael a sidelong look. It was dark out, but a streetlight revealed his wrinkled face and kind eyes.

"I'm not sure what I'm saying. But I can tell he's afraid of losing you. He's afraid you are Janet number two and that he fell in love with a woman whose heart will never truly be in Sweetheart Creek or with him."

She nodded. That much had become apparent during their conversation.

"I should have been more forthcoming about what I have going on away from here," she sighed.

But at the same time she'd wanted to ignore it all, preferring to get caught up in the dream of his wonderful world, where everything seemed to make sense and nothing else existed unless she wanted it to.

Now it looked as though she might not get to enter that world, because in the process she'd broken his faith in her.

***

LEVI SPENT Thursday morning working around the ranch, righting rain barrels, fixing holes in the turf made by the stampede, having Laura's car towed to the wrecker's at Clint's recommendation, and trying to ignore a growing sense of unease. Brant had returned Lupe, stating that his front leg was just bruised, not broken.

Last night's fiasco wasn't something that would have a lasting impact on the ranch, even though Levi was certain it was making the gossip rounds. Especially with the stampede photo and article in a New York newspaper, courtesy of the reporter who'd been in attendance last night. Henry had stopped by to wave the paper in Levi's face, proclaiming that Laura didn't belong on the ranch. The reporter had captured it all in black-and-white—the stampede, Laura, Levi—and he'd dished out more information about their private lives than Levi felt the public should be privy to.

But it was the quote from Laura, about feeling it was too late to have kids, and that she wanted to travel the world, that had set him back. This article wasn't in a tabloid. Was it the truth? If so, why hadn't she told him? Had Sweetheart Creek just been her lightning-strike stopover, and now that she knew what she wanted, she was gone? Gone back to glitz and glamor and everything he and the ranch were not?

It had all felt like more than that to him.

Levi walked into the stable where Laura was slowly hanging up the last of the equipment, the riders having left almost forty minutes ago.

He didn't try to kiss her, keeping his distance. Last night's conversation about the future had left too many questions swirling in his mind.

"The photo shoot date got moved up," she said, crouching to pet Lupe. She crooned over him, her guilt for his injury obvious. It didn't help that the dog seemed to exaggerate his mild limp in front of her. "We're aiming to avoid a possible incoming hurricane for the outdoor part of the shoot."

"When do you go?"

"Tomorrow."

"But…" He glanced around the stable. She was going to leave him high and dry with the riders?

"Myles said he'd step in for me. And honestly, it's probably for the best. Betty called and said Wilma found out about the scholarship and is upset. She's pulling Donnie from lessons. But she said it wasn't just the humiliation of being seen as a charity case, but also because she felt he wasn't safe here with me. Two other riders canceled their lessons for the week, as well. The community is losing faith in me."

"Stampedes happen. If I'd known that reporter was going to tear us up I would have kicked him out."

Laura wouldn't look at him and he could sense the hurt she was trying to hide. "Reporters are going to be snooping around here more after last night's show. Me going away for a week is probably for the best."

A week. Why did that feel as if it was going to be a lot longer?

"Where will you stay?"

"A hotel in South Carolina. Then when we move to the studio in New York I'll stay at my sister's."

"You're coming back?"

Laura stepped closer, watching him. She looked exhausted, as though she'd barely slept last night. "Yes. I plan to come back."

He let out a breath of relief. "What day?"

"I'm not sure yet."

"Thursday? Friday?"

"I don't know. There's the outdoor shoot, which is weather dependent, then we head to the city. While we're finishing up there I'll sign some contracts with my agent and lawyer. Sometimes they go fast, sometimes they take eons. These types of deals are new for me so it could get complicated."

"Lawyers and agents," Levi mused. "My cowgirl princess has lawyers and agents."

"Yes, Levi. I'm a businesswoman. A model. A celebrity. A public brand out there selling stuff. This woman isn't a true cowgirl. She hasn't earned her boots, and I think yesterday proved that."

His head snapped up. "I think she's all of the above. She's just spent less time as one of them. Making mistakes is part of earning your boots."

"I bought the wrong boots because they looked pretty."

"I happen to like that about you." It felt as if he was losing her, as if she was looking for excuses not to be here, a place he could tell she loved. He couldn't let yesterday's debacle or the newspaper stories drive her away. She belonged here. They both did.

"You need to know that I don't do long-distance," he reminded her gruffly.

"I can't ignore this contract because you want me to, Levi."

"I'm not asking you to. I'm asking you to tell me if you're going to be away a long time."

Laura's jaw slackened. "I said I'll be a week."

"I love you. I didn't mean to, but I do." He sucked in a deep breath. "And if you don't want kids then I can figure it out."

"What?"

"As for travel, I haven't been many places. The ranch takes up a lot of my time."

"What are you talking about?"

"You're not just a warm body fixing a problem. I know you're not homeless or running away or buying your way into the town's favor."

She inhaled slowly. "You believed the article?" She looked indignant.

He shrugged. "I just thought maybe you'd—"

"I was honest with *you*."

"You didn't tell me about this photo shoot even though you knew it was coming. You sold the house when it wasn't even listed. You told me you were retired. Is it so wrong to think that maybe it's true that you can't have kids or don't want them?"

"You think I was just telling you things you wanted to hear?"

Wow, this was twisting up faster than a calf caught in a sloppily tossed lasso. There were tears in her eyes and he wasn't exactly sure why they were there, only that his words had caused them and that the right ones would make them dry up.

"No, I don't think that."

"I have always had a life outside of Texas. I thought you were on board with me having a world beyond you and this ranch."

"I thought you were retired! I thought you were staying!"

"I am!"

"You're not! My home is here and you're leaving." His jaw tightened. "I'm trying to be understanding, but the truth is that women who like the high life don't come back to Sweetheart Creek, Laura."

"One woman left you. One."

"I'm not leaving Texas."

"I didn't ask you to."

"Exactly."

evi checked the scrap of paper again, then looked up at the building in front of him. City addresses confused him. Did the building's address correlate to the street it was located on, or the crossroad? He shifted his hat farther back on his head and tried to pick out which window might be Laura's sister's.

The city smelled. While walking down the city blocks, he'd stepped in bubblegum, caught the aromas of sewers, exhaust and a million different kinds of food, and he hadn't seen a green thing or a bird since he'd gotten on the plane in Texas.

But he was here. And according to the unanswered apartment buzzer, Laura was not.

She'd been gone a full week, and when she'd texted to say she'd be a few more days in New York he'd climbed on a plane to find out if she was ever coming back.

He stepped away from the intercom and pulled out his cell phone. He could call her. Would she pick up? Be happy to see him? Think he was paranoid and didn't trust that she would keep her word?

Levi went back outside and sat on the front railing, watching traffic and pedestrians go by as he contemplated his next move. Finally, about an hour later, he was rewarded by the sight of a familiar face heading his way: Laura's. She was walking with a man wearing a smart-looking suit and tie.

Laura was laughing, her shiny hair flowing behind her in waves as she strode along, her short skirt and high heels making her legs look incredibly long and strong. There was no trace of the cowgirl he'd known only last week; she was every bit the model, from her polished toenails to her bright red lipstick, to the stylish sweater sliding off one shoulder.

Levi pushed away from the railing and Laura's steps faltered. Then she hitched her bright red bag higher and picked up speed, sending him a smile. A big one, just for him, and his heart lifted.

She turned back briefly, saying goodbye to the man she'd been walking with, pausing long enough to give him an air kiss, as well as receive one on each cheek.

As Laura approached Levi, he said, "Thought maybe you'd be available for supper?"

With her all dolled up it was difficult to equate this version of Laura to the one he'd fallen for.

She was a few feet away and she stopped, her expression cautious. "You came here to ask me out to supper?"

"I did."

She smiled again, her chin lowered bashfully. "That's really romantic, you know."

"I miss you."

She came closer, gave him a light kiss. "I miss you, too."

He caught her by the elbow, keeping her near. There was a sadness in her eyes he couldn't explain.

He released her elbow and stepped back with a sigh. "I can't eat. I can't sleep. Please come home."

Her eyes filled with regret, but there was a firm determination as well. Her chin lifted as she said, "I'm in the middle of making deals. I need to be here."

He hooked his hand in hers, knowing she was firm on staying.

"I need to be here just like you need to be in Texas—solving all of your family's ranch problems."

"I *have* to be there," Levi insisted.

"Last I heard that ranch was owned by five different people."

He jerked as though stung. "My brothers are figuring out their lives right now. Building their futures."

"So am I."

"You said you were retired, and now you're neck deep in modeling and staying here, looking like this." He lifted his hat and scratched his forehead. She was gorgeous, but almost unrecognizable. Which Laura was real, his or this one? "Are you coming back?"

"Quit asking me that! I said I am. Just…there's more to me than the ranch. I know it's the center of your world, and I love the place and everything about it, but I really need you to not get weird about the time I have to spend here right now."

"I told you I don't do long-distance relationships."

Her tone changed, becoming cool and careful. "If I'm not helping out on the ranch is there still a place for me in your life?"

Of course. But she didn't belong here, in this place she called home. He could see it in her eyes, in the way her shoulders tensed as they spoke. Home shouldn't do that to a person.

She was blinking hard, as if she'd been caught in a dirt devil and needed to flush her eyes.

He had a whole speech prepared about how she could live on the ranch and do her New York stuff from there, or fly back to the city as needed. Now all he could see was how different they were.

She reached out and grasped his arms, her large bag sliding down to her elbow. "Levi, I care a great deal for you." Her voice had softened, as though that might make her words hurt less. "But if you're looking for a woman who is going to stay on the ranch every day, that's not me."

"You're looking for the princess life, is that it?" He stepped back, breaking her hold. "You want pretty things? Cowboy boots that hurt your feet?"

Her nostrils flared and her jaw tightened. "I thought I was looking for and had found a new home, a community and a man who loved me for who I am. I guess I was wrong."

LAURA STOOD at the window in her sister's apartment watching the empty street, her heart aching. What had she done? Why hadn't she just thrown everything to the wind and followed Levi back to Texas?

Because he wanted you to live as a cowgirl in his world, and that was just like Memphis wanting you to keep being a model here in New York.

She needed someone who understood and was willing to accommodate the changes in her life.

But why did this hurt worse than losing Memphis? Her relationship with Levi had been so much shorter.

Laura opened her massive purse and took out a file folder thick with contracts. She had her work cut out for her, and the sooner she got lost in it all, the sooner she could forget Levi and the distinct urge to start sobbing and never stop.

As she sat on the couch Target jumped up beside her.

"Hey, little friend." Brant had allowed her to adopt Target, and she'd taken him to a few obedience classes already. So far he was proving to be a fast learner, and he'd been good about air travel, as well as staying in the apartment during the day. She'd even registered him in a ranch-dog school back in Texas, but it looked like she could cancel that one.

By the time the apartment was dark enough that she needed to turn on a light, Laura heard a key in the lock, her heart beginning to pound. Nobody had a key but her and her sister. And Ava was in Taiwan.

"I thought you were supposed to be gone for another two weeks!" Laura said, jumping to her feet to go hug Ava.

"Took a long weekend. Red-eye flights. Don't ask." Ava dropped her suitcase with a clunk and kicked the door shut, giving Laura a tight hug. "I figured if you're still in New York instead of Texas something bad must have happened."

Laura let out a shaky laugh as she released her sister, stating, "Nothing bad's happened."

"You're lying. You're tucking your hair behind your ear, and you just crossed your arms."

Laura uncrossed them. "People can do those things, you know."

"And you just lifted your chin. It's even worse than I thought." Ava opened her arms to give Laura a second hug, Target bouncing off both of them.

"I sent him away," Laura said.

"Your dog is cute, but he's not listening to your command to go away. He's currently climbing my leg. You might want to look into how much you're paying for that training you've been texting about."

"No. Levi was here. He was waiting outside the building when I got home from the lawyer's office."

Her sister held her at arm's length. "What do you mean, Levi was here?" She bent and scooped up Target. "Hey, cutie. Nice to meet you in person."

"He came to New York to ask me out for supper." Laura swiped at her wet cheeks.

"He left his ranch?" her sister asked in surprise.

"And took the time to get a haircut." Laura felt the tears start up in earnest. It was just a haircut.

"The ranch. The place you said he'd never, ever leave, not for anything in the world. And he flew all the way to New York. Asked you to dinner. And you sent him away?"

Laura nodded, feeling even more uncertain about what she'd done.

"What did he do to you?"

"He just…" Laura sniffled and waved her hands helplessly. "I caused a stampede. Things won't work out with me on the ranch, and people are mad about the scholarship and say I'm throwing my money around to make everyone like me. The whole community has lost faith in me."

"Yeah, yeah. Whine, whine. Blame yourself for everything," she said while scratching Target under the chin. "Get to the part about the man."

"I just don't see how we can live our lives together. He wants me in Texas on his ranch, playing cowgirl, and I failed at that." She slumped in defeat. "I didn't even buy the right kind of cowboy boots."

"But you seemed happy." Her sister released Target, who was eager to go sniff her suitcase, then flopped onto the couch, her face creased.

Outside, the noise of sirens grew louder, then faded away. Laura missed the sound of birds, and how people would meet her eye and nod at her on the street. She had formed the habit quickly in Sweetheart Creek, freaking people out when she'd returned to New York and continued to do so. She'd noticed how they all gave her a wide berth, as though she was crazy, or about to ask them for something they didn't want to give.

"I don't need another man trying to keep me in one place because he can't handle me changing and being different than his perception of me."

Her sister got up, came over and embraced her again. "Oh, honey. Memphis left you with issues, you know that?"

"Levi wants me to stay on the ranch because his ex left for Hollywood and didn't come back. It's like I'm a repeat for him."

"And vice versa. You feel he's a repeat of Memphis being resentful of the time you spent on your career. That's why we have rebound relationships—to clean our emotional house before we go off and find the real deal."

Ava whisked a tissue from the box kept on the nearby end table. She held it out for Laura while giving her a meaningful look that implied she felt Levi was the real deal, and that Laura had just blown it by using him like a rebound to get over Memphis. Laura accepted the tissue and wiped her nose.

"But it sounds like your issues and Levi's are keeping you from having what could be a very good thing. So how do you get past that?"

"It would be stupid to run after him to the airport, wouldn't it?"

"Yes, it would. First of all, you don't know which airport he's flying out of, not to mention which airline he's on, correct? Secondly, there's this invention called the cell phone. I'm pretty sure even cowboys have them."

Laura shook her head, collapsing onto the couch in turn. "I can't call him."

"Why not?"

"I can't see either of us changing our paths right now. He belongs there and I belong..." Where? She didn't know any longer. She wanted to belong in Sweetheart Creek, but wasn't sure she had the courage to go back and face everyone while working her way back into the fold.

"So you don't love him?"

"What? I do!"

"I thought you liked working in the stables."

"I do."

"So?"

"There's more to me than that woman, and it's like that's all he's willing to see. I can't give up who I am, and I know he feels the same way about his own life."

"So it's better to give up now?"

"Yes! He belongs there, and it wouldn't be fair to ask him to leave. But I need to be here. It's obvious our lives are bigger than our love for each other." She wiped her eyes again, her chest aching.

Her sister pulled a printed-out receipt off the coffee table and waved it at her. "Except he just came all the way across the country to see you. And you apparently enrolled Target in how-to-be-a-ranch-dog school." Her sister dropped the receipt on the table. "Quit being scared and figure it out. You only get a shot at true love once. Don't blow it."

LEVI KICKED a bale as he strode through the back stable on the ranch. He had flown all the way to New York for nothing.

What had he been thinking? Of course she'd refused him.

Her and those red lips and high heels, and that sexy sweater slipping off her shoulder.

He was not doing long-distance.

He was not moving to New York.

And she didn't care. She hadn't even asked him to.

He slammed the door to the small storage room a little too hard, hearing wood crack. He mixed up a bottle for the lamb, wishing it didn't remind him of how natural Laura had been with the animal, taking over the task while she was here.

He should have kept searching for a replacement for Betty, shouldn't have eased up. He'd known Laura was going to leave, but he'd put on blinders because of how happy he'd been, when the truth from lessons learned was sitting there in front of him the whole time.

The bottle ready, he stormed back out of the storage room and nearly ran into Brant and Myles.

"Whoa," Myles said. "What's your deal?"

"I don't have a deal," Levi muttered, pushing past him.

Myles grabbed his arm and spun him around. "Seriously? What's your problem?" he challenged.

Levi tensed, ready to fight. "I don't have a problem."

"Yeah, you do."

"Come on, guys," Brant stated, stepping between them.

"Everyone knows why you're in a bad mood," Myles said. "She was always out of your league. Get over it."

"What do you know about someone being out of your league?"

Myles lifted his chin. "Plenty."

Brant said gently, "I know you're hurting because she left—"

"Shut up. What do you know about women leaving?"

Brant gave a shrug. "Nothing. Plenty. Your pick."

Women didn't leave Brant. They loved how he was their best friend. If he wanted to get married all he had to do was stand up in the diner and make the announcement, and he'd be hitched by noon.

"You know nothing," Levi growled.

"You need to get over her, because everybody's tired of you crashing around breaking things," Brant said.

Levi glared at him. "I'll get over it when I feel like it."

"Or you could move to New York," Brant suggested. "Learn how relationships require both give and take."

Give and take? He'd done plenty of both.

"And who would take care of the ranch?" he challenged. "You?"

"Sure."

"You're going to solve all the problems around here?"

"Considering you fabricate most of them, yeah."

"Do you understand all that I do around here?"

"She's not coming back," Myles muttered. "And why should she? You're impossible."

"Am I?"

"Yeah. Your head is so far up your butt you only see yourself."

"Says you."

Myles shifted to face Levi. "You only wanted to see her as was a cowgirl. Well, open your eyes, bro. She's so much more than that. She's a celebrity! She's got stuff going on none of us can even begin to understand."

"Did you know she's brokering a few million-dollar deals in New York right now?" Brant narrowed his eyes, making Levi feel self-absorbed for not knowing.

"It's all based on the reputation and brand she's built up as a model," Brant explained patiently. "Not as a cowgirl. She's at a point in her career where she's ready to sit back and make bank."

"Make bank?"

"Mullah. Lots of it. Set for life."

"If she loved me…" Wouldn't that be more important than money?

"How about if *you* loved *her*?"

"You know why she left?" he said, not wanting to think about Brant's question.

Myles and Brant both looked at him.

"She left because of you." Levi pointed at Brant accusingly. "Why did you buy her aunt's house? Why do you need possession right away? You have a home. You wanted to drive her out of town because you're jealous she chose me. This is just like you, and—"

"You think you know everything," Brant interrupted, his expression closed.

"I know you sent her away."

"You knew she was going to break your heart," he said quietly. "Unfortunately, I think you broke hers, too."

"Thanks to you. We didn't even get a chance to figure things out."

"She deserves better than some guy expecting her to give up her entire life and move down here so she can be the wife you've always wanted. That's selfish." Brant's voice softened. "Why would you try to change the very things you love most about her?"

"What do you know about love?"

He crossed his arms, leaning back. "Considering I just bought a house for someone, I'd say I know a darn lot."

Brant pivoted, marching away, with Myles on his heels. They left Levi feeling more confused than ever.

LEVI DIDN'T ENJOY it when his brothers were right. He *had* expected Laura to fit into his life without any references to her former life as a model. Sure, he'd thought her retirement meant she was completely done with that world, but he hadn't asked, had he? Even his granddad, also retired, still consulted on problems affecting the ranch. It made sense that Laura wouldn't be retiring cold turkey. Levi should have been more accommodating, instead of letting his fears override reason.

He'd expected her to move here and live *his* life. Which was nothing but the ranch.

It had been a long time since he'd been in a relationship, and he'd forgotten that there were two sides to everything, two dreams, two sets of emotions, two people, two lives.

Maybe that was part of his problem with his brother Cole. When the second-born Wylder had run into issues, Levi had been there to support him, sure. But had he been a good listener? He had a feeling he'd pushed his own solutions on Cole instead of giving him time and space to fix things his own way.

In other words, Levi was the problem.

He shook his head and checked the time. Lots of hours left in the day to begin making changes. And he might as well start with Cole, because if he could patch things with him, then maybe he'd free up enough time to try and fix things with Laura. Assuming she wasn't completely done with him.

Levi took the all-terrain vehicle from the machine shed and drove out through the irrigated pasture, then on beyond to one that was more dry, heading toward the waterfall he had claimed as his own. Continuing on, he forded the creek where, as teens, he and his brothers, along with April, had thrown rock after rock into the water to create a shallower crossing point. The sun dipped behind a fluffy cloud when he finally crested the hill and spotted Brant near windmill five. He was sitting on the railing that protected the windmill's gearbox from rubbing cattle, looking out over the meadow, his back to the calves he'd claimed he'd come out to check on.

Feeling as though he was intruding on his brother's personal meditation, Levi slowed the machine. Hearing the engine, Brant turned, and Levi noted how his shoulders tightened as though he was bracing himself. Levi parked the ATV near Brant's truck with its veterinary clinic logo and cut the engine. "I'm sorry I've been as moody as a stuck cow," he said.

His brother didn't reply, just watched him from under the brim of his hat.

"You were right. It was my fault. Not just with Laura, but with Cole, too."

Brant pushed his hat back, studying Levi.

"Do you know where he is?" Levi asked. "I think maybe I need to call and apologize."

"I thought you had."

It had been several years since his last attempt. In retrospect, it probably hadn't been the best apology. "I think I could do better."

"And you think I have his number?"

"I'm hoping so."

Brant was quiet for a long moment. "You going to demand he comes back to the ranch to figure everything out?"

"Yep."

Brant shook his head. "You're a slow learner, aren't you?"

"And you've never really understood a joke."

"Maybe I didn't find that one particularly funny."

"I'll work on my punch lines."

His brother was being unnaturally difficult—his way of protecting someone. Myles brought out the fists, Ryan his smarts, and Brant just plain old unhelpfulness.

Brant leaned sideways, digging into his back pocket. He fished out his phone and started typing, and a few seconds later Levi heard a familiar sound as the message he'd sent came through. He looked at his screen. Cole's contact information. That had been so easy he felt a wash of shame for not trying sooner.

"You know," Brant said, "I didn't buy Luanne's house to make things difficult between you and Laura."

Levi wasn't ready to talk about that. How was he supposed to get to know a woman when she lived hundreds of miles away? Her having a house here had been perfect. And in today's market it would have taken a long time to sell if it hadn't been for his meddlesome brother.

"Who did you buy it for?" he asked.

Brant stood, heading to his truck.

"I'm going to find out who your secret girlfriend is when she moves in."

"Call Cole. Talk to him."

"Don't change the subject."

"Maybe I'm not," Brant said easily, frustrating Levi even further.

"What does that mean?"

"What are you going to do about Laura?"

Dodging topics. There was definitely something going on with Brant. Levi forced himself to let it go. Not every problem was his to solve, even though he was itching to get to the bottom of this one.

"You know we have to figure out the ranch situation," Levi said. "The way we're running things isn't sustainable."

"Talk to Cole, and we'll take the conversation from there."

"Okay."

"And seriously? You need to apologize to Laura."

LAURA SAT in her agent's office while Reina Riley talked to someone out in the hall. Laura had signed the contract to start her own perfume line, and had accepted several of the proposed scents to claim as her own. The plan was to spend the next hour hashing out details around their branding and marketing.

She was exhausted from the shoot, followed by contract negotiations and her breakup with Levi. Because that's what it had been, hadn't it? They hadn't spoken since.

The worst part was that Ava was right. Laura was hiding out, afraid to take a chance with Levi, and what felt like true love. But how could she go back when she'd been so bad at keeping the ranch safe? Yes, accidents happened, but there was truth behind Wilma's worries about Donnie's safety with her there, especially with her being so new to it all.

As Laura flipped through the marketing proposals, the glossy images seemed even more fake and posed than usual. Something had changed in her since she'd spent time in Texas. She wanted to take the airbrushed models and make them look more down-home, more genuine and appealing to the average woman.

If only she could capture the feeling she'd had in the stables the time Levi had helped her brush down the horses after a riding session. They had been standing side by side and he had leaned closer, inhaling her scent, his nose buried in her neck. She had giggled and he'd caught her in his arms, making her feel more cherished and beautiful than any of the times she'd gone to balls or galas. She wanted to give that feeling to her customers. And these glitzy photos couldn't do that.

"Laura?" Reina sat opposite her, snapping Laura out of her reverie. "What do you think? Anything grab your attention?"

Laura glanced down at the folder of glamorous images and label mockups she was holding. "What do you think about a perfume for the average woman?"

"Aren't all perfumes for the average woman?" Reina perched her glasses on top of her streaked gray hair. "We're just selling them the dream of being something more."

That was what spending time with Levi had given her. The dream that she could shed her old life and live something new.

"That's why you're going to be the one in all the ads," Reina continued. "Not some random model. You."

"But what if we offered an image of an everyday woman? A real one with charming but imperfect features, rather than someone fake and made up?"

"What do you mean?" Reina asked carefully.

"What about if we offered a cowgirl?"

"That's not your brand."

"No, not yet. My brand is every other model's brand." To stand out would amount to risk. "But what if we had beautiful women in everyday lives? An executive being powerful in the boardroom, a mom busy at home, maybe a vet working with dogs?"

"I don't know that this is our market. Perfume isn't as on trend as it once was, what with no-scent zones becoming more common."

"Then why are we making perfume?"

"Because it's what we've always done."

"Maybe we could do footwear. Cowboy boots that feel good?" she said with a laugh.

"Perfume has an amazing markup. Footwear is more costly to produce and can be very hit and miss. To be truthful, we are even a bit late getting out there with this perfume. We should have done it at your peak. We're going to have to work hard. No slacking off or risk-taking. Get our money and get out."

"So we go glossy?"

"We go glossy."

They spent the next hour working on a common vision and making notes to send to the marketing and product development teams.

"Is there much more you need from me before the next meeting?" Laura stood, sliding the straps of her bag over her shoulder. "I think I need to get out of town for a few days."

"We're good for the time being." Reina's expression turned to one of concern. "I'm sorry about your aunt. Are things going okay with the house?"

"I sold it."

"That was fast."

"I know."

"Are you okay?"

"Yeah."

"I don't mean to be nosy, but you haven't seemed yourself since coming back."

"I'm just not sure New York's still for me. There's a lot here, but I might..." She scrunched her nose, embarrassed for expressing her half-cooked thoughts. "Oh, I don't know. I thought I'd found something, but then I messed up and now everything feels off."

"It's normal to feel as though you're at a crossroads with your career right now. Maybe a little lost, too?"

Laura nodded.

"The only advice I can offer is to not do anything rash."

"Such as fall in love with a cowboy down in Texas and consider leaving New York behind?"

Reina raised her eyebrows and tucked her chin on top of her hands, elbows on her desk, all ears. "My, my. Tell me more. But please don't say you plan to be in breach of any of these lovely contracts we've signed this week." She gave a light laugh.

"I won't. I know what my goals are."

"So?"

"So I played cowgirl for a few weeks while I was sorting out the house. It was fun."

"And?"

"There was this cowboy…" Laura found herself sitting again. "He thought I was amazing and we had an incredible connection, but then I screwed up, and we realized we were seeing things differently in our relationship. It all ended on a sour note."

"And? The problem is…?"

"I'm not equipped to be a cowgirl."

"Did you get stepped on by a horse?" Reina asked, her tone becoming more businesslike.

"What? No. Didn't you hear about the stampede?"

"An honest accident by the sound of things. And nobody got hurt."

"Luckily."

"Did a saddle fall off a horse?"

"No. Why?"

"Did you run a horse into a barbed-wire fence or fall down a well?"

Laura laughed. "No."

"Then you probably did better as a cowgirl than you think."

"I let my puppy loose in the stables and spooked the horses. Left a gate open and Target—my dog—got free and caused a stampede right through Levi's birthday party."

Laura held back a giggle. It sounded so ridiculous. How was she still blaming herself for all this?

Because it was embarrassing and had been preventable.

But it was also something to hide behind, so she didn't have to think about how much she cared for Levi.

"Since when do you have a puppy?"

"I began fostering one while I was there." Because Brant thought she was family. So had Levi.

She felt her eyes prick with tears. She missed them, missed the community, even though she knew she'd get teased about the stampede for the rest of her life if she returned.

"I adopted the dog. And I started a scholarship."

"You did?" Reina smiled.

She explained what it was for and how some felt she was throwing her money around.

"Oh, that happens everywhere."

Laura frowned.

"Honey, how many times have nasties spilled drinks on your gown at galas? It's the same horse poop, different pile. It's jealousy. Feelings of inadequacy. You've held your head up high through worse."

"I also bought pretty cowboy boots instead of practical ones," she whispered.

"Darling, you're a woman, are you not?" When Laura gave her a blank look, Reina continued, "Have I not trained all practicality out of you? Give yourself a break. I'm pretty good, you know."

Laura laughed. "That's true."

Her agent leaned forward again. "You remember when you were that crazy-haired, crooked-toothed kid? Who taught you how to dress? If you had bought ugly but practical boots, you know I would've marched all the way down to Texas and complained about how you were ruining your image and brand."

Laura laughed again. Reina always knew how to give her the right perspective to feel better.

"Learning new things isn't easy. Remember your first modeling gig?"

She had tossed a discarded shirt over a floodlamp and set the whole backdrop on fire.

"We all make newbie errors. Right? And everyone was okay in the end."

She nodded as they stood, Reina pulling her into a big hug.

"Get away for a few days," she said into Laura's ear, "Head down to Texas and see where things are at."

When they broke apart, Laura fiddled with the zipper on her purse. "I don't know. I still have to clear out the last few things from my aunt's house and sign some papers, but that's only going to take me a day."

"And?"

"And as of next week I won't have anywhere to stay down there."

"But you want to stay?"

"Levi… He's the one I fell for." A familiar warmth flowed through her as she spoke his name. "Our lives are so different…"

"Isn't there an expression about how love conquers all?"

Laura frowned at her.

"I won't need you for anything for at least a week and a half. Maybe longer. Anything that comes up I can email to you, or we can talk on the phone." Reina walked her to the door. "Go to Texas. Talk to Levi. Figure this out. I will not have you moping around when I need a smiling, happy woman when we go talk to various execs about this line. Understood?"

She did. She just wasn't sure that talking to Levi was going to help.

*L*evi sat on a hay bale at the edge of the dance floor, arms crossed. Why had he allowed Brant to drag him to the barn dance, anyway? He had no intention of getting out there. And why did Myles keep eyeing the cheerleading manager, Karen Hartley. She was dressed in Western gear, her shirt buttoned to her chin as if to illustrate that she was more librarian than cowgirl. So far it didn't seem as though Myles had done more than give her a smile and a nod from his spot manning the door and the donation jar.

"You gonna dance?" Brant asked, taking a sip from his plastic cup. "Or are you going to sit there all night with a foul look on your face?"

"Sit here." He had things on his mind.

"Now there's a face as foul as yours," Brant said, as their grandfather stalked by.

"What are you looking at?" Carmichael asked, his semi-permanent scowl in place.

"Nothing much," Levi replied.

Carmichael came to a halt, his thumbs in his belt loops. "You know, I was going to tell you how proud I am of the way you've been taking care of the ranch, but never mind."

"What?" Brant and Levi said at the same time.

"You can take your sassy attitude and live alone for the rest of your life for all I care. I was going to admit you boys have turned out not half-bad. I'll save myself the trouble." He continued on, grimacing to hide what could be a different emotion. Brant and Levi looked at each other and shrugged.

"He half hugged me when I graduated from veterinary school," Brant said. "I thought he was dying."

Levi smirked. He would have likely thought the same thing.

Seeing Ryan chatting with Myles out front, Levi and Brant wandered over to join them.

"I can't get ahold of Cole," Levi told his brothers by way of hello.

"Why not?" Brant asked.

"The number was no good."

"Really?" Ryan asked, doubt lacing his voice.

"Must be. He didn't pick up."

Brant gave him a slow, assessing look that echoed Ryan's earlier tone. Cole was avoiding his call.

"Anyway," Levi continued, "I'm done waiting for him to return, and I'm done with the ranch being the only thing in my life."

While he didn't know what he would do with any freed-up time, especially without Laura around, he had come to realize just how much he had been missing out by burying himself in running the ranch.

"What?" Brant turned to face him, eyes wide.

Levi gathered his thoughts, realizing he was worrying his brothers. He had planned to call an official Wylder meeting to discuss his thoughts and plans for the ranch and his own future, but he found he wanted this off his chest now. No more waiting. No more trying to do it all.

"I still love it, and I'm keeping my share and will continue to run it," he stated.

Brant visibly relaxed, as did Myles.

"I'm also ready to buy out you four if that's what you want." The banker hadn't found his idea to be brilliant, but it was potentially doable. "I'm also hiring help. I've been hearing good things about Owen Lancaster, and I'm prepared to make him an offer if nobody objects. Myles, Hank and I can't do it all."

Myles nodded. "You have my vote for hiring Owen. And I'd like to keep my share, if that's all right with you, Levi."

"Of course," Levi said, clapping Myles on the shoulder. "I'd be lost without you."

"If we can afford Owen, I'm in. But we'll have to sort out what exactly you need from me in terms of time spent on the ranch," Brant said, lifting his hat to push a hand through his hair. "But I do know I don't want to lose the ranch, or my share."

"Fair enough," Levi said. "Your veterinarian expertise helps us out tremendously, and saves us a lot on vet bills. We'll figure something out."

"How much help do you expect us to provide?" Ryan asked, glancing toward Carmichael, who was leaning against a post inside, shooting the breeze with a friend. They were all aware that every outside hire impacted Carmichael's retirement fund. But so did neglecting the work that needed to be done.

"I'm not sure yet. If y'all want to step up more, or try some new stuff to increase the ranch's profits, I'm game. But unless you're working on the ranch full-time, I have the final call on everything and I'm going to be making some changes. I'm already considering possible alterations to our calving schedule to increase our success rate. And income, by lowering winter feed costs. That said, the ranch isn't everyone's slush fund any longer. You work or contribute in other ways, you keep your share. You don't want to do your part, I buy you out."

Ryan was looking thoughtful, nodding. "Sounds fair."

"Figure out exactly how you see things working out for you and the ranch, and within the next four weeks we'll set things down in stone, or I'll start drawing up the buyout contracts."

His brothers mulled that over in silence.

April MacFarlane came up with her four-year-old son, Kurt. Brant and Levi tipped their hats and the serious young boy did the same. April juggled her casserole for the potluck while she dug in her purse for some donation money, and the men gave Kurt high fives and asked about the toy tractor he was carrying. Mother and son entered the barn, and moments later April's husband, Heath Thompson, came jogging up. He tipped his hat at the men with a friendly smile, his large rodeo championship belt buckle winking under the light shining down from above the barn doors.

"April paid?" he asked.

"Yup," Myles said, before the man headed inside to meet up with his wife, giving her a kiss on the cheek.

"I thought Mom said their marriage was on the rocks," Levi said in a low voice.

Brant shrugged and took a sip of his soda.

They watched April and Heath join the line dance, smiling as their blue-eyed son did his best to keep up.

When Travis Nestner, the mayor, showed up to take over Myles's post manning the door, the Wylder brothers wandered inside, Myles and Ryan heading over to the tables laden with potluck offerings. Levi watched as Myles's ex-girlfriend Daisy-Mae Ray tracked him, flirting and looking for attention, which Myles studiously ignored. It seemed as though the Wylder brothers were going to be single for a very long time at this rate.

"Look who's here," Brant said under his breath a few moments later.

"Don't try and distract me from being miserable," Levi muttered.

"You might want to be distracted by this." Brant stepped aside so that Levi had a clear view of the doorway.

His mind went blank. It was Laura, returning Mrs. Fisher's welcoming embrace. She was wearing a straw cowboy hat, a checkered shirt tied in a knot at her navel, the cute denim skirt she'd worn to the football game, and those ridiculous, utterly impracticable blue cowboy boots. She came their way, tall and strong and every bit the gorgeous woman he'd fallen for. No red lipstick. No fancy city clothes.

He stepped forward, asking, "What do you have about those dang boots, anyway?"

She twisted her foot, looking at them. "They're pretty. Not ones I would wear in the stables anymore, but they're great on a night like this. Besides, I heard that someone here likes the fact that I chose these impractical boots."

Him. She was flirting. And possibly trying to pick up where they had left off. But Levi couldn't quite reconcile the two versions of Laura he knew. The woman he'd fallen for and the one who had a glitzy life far away from Sweetheart Creek.

"Why are you here?" he asked, wishing it sounded less like a demand. They hadn't spoken to each other since a week ago in New York. She couldn't just waltz—or two-step—back into his arms.

He needed her. Not just in the stables, but in his life. And for lots more than when she had a few days available here and there.

"Well, I do have a home in Texas." She looked up at him with bright eyes. "At least for another few days." She glanced at Brant, who immediately smiled and turned away, leaving them together after a quick tip of his hat. "I also feel a bit silly wearing this hat in New York," Laura added. "Same with the boots."

"I'm sure they're not the silliest things you've ever worn." He meant it as a joke, but she didn't laugh, just turned to watch the dancers.

Myles was chatting with Karen now. The librarian wasn't

even close to the type Myles normally gravitated toward, and it was beginning to look as though Brant wasn't the only Wylder with a secret life these days.

Levi turned to speak to Laura just as she began to speak as well.

"You first," he said.

"I was going to ask how the stables have been."

"Fine." Realizing he was shutting down the conversation, he added, "My mom moved a tiny home into the yard. She said there was no way she was moving back into the bedroom she'd shared with my father." He meant it jokingly, but there was tension in his voice that Laura caught. She reached out, gently laying a hand on his arm.

"I'm glad she's back."

He gave a sharp nod. "Me, too."

They stared out at the dancers for an awkward moment.

"Do you want to dance?" Laura asked.

Levi didn't take time to consider, but swept her into his arms and across the dance floor.

"You're still a horrible dancer," he said, when she stepped on his left foot.

"Maybe I need someone to help me get more practice. I hear these dances are held fairly frequently."

"They're a long way from New York."

"I was thinking I could rent a place in town while I decide where I'm going to live next."

His head snapped up. "Why would you do that?"

"The rent's cheap." He could see her swallow, looking slightly apprehensive, as though she was expecting to get hurt. He'd made her feel that way.

He slipped his hand from her waist to the small of her back. "Any other reason?" he asked gently.

"A man I met suggested I stick around and spend some time getting to know him. I enjoyed the time we shared, even though

I'll never quite be the cowgirl he'd like me to be." She met his eyes. "We have different lives and I'm not sure how things will work out, but I love him too much to just walk away without trying."

"You know, Brant was saying something the other day." He automatically glanced toward his brother, who was now chatting with April, deep in conversation like the best friend he'd always been. She was pressing a hand to his arm, looking earnest and amused. That man sure was a good listener, and he made Levi realize he could do a better job of it himself.

"What did he say?" Laura asked.

Levi focused on her again. "You should love a person for who they truly are, not for the image you have in your head."

"What does that mean?"

He gave a shrug. "Beats me."

She rewarded him with a laugh and he spun her into a twirl, just about losing her as the unexpected move took her off guard. He swept her back against him, steadying her.

"I'd like to get to know you," he said, growing more serious. "The real you. The one with lawyers and agents and big fancy deals, and who has to take off sometimes." He swallowed hard. "As long as you keep coming back."

"That woman doesn't feel like the real me when I'm here. I shut her out last time. I shouldn't have, because in some way it also meant shutting you and our future out."

"She's a big part of you."

"And so was that fumbling cowgirl."

"You weren't fumbling."

"Levi…" she said gently.

"I know you think I'm overselling your skills, but that lamb trusted you, those kids and horses, too." He started moving again and she fell into step, swaying slowly. "I trust you, Laura. And you seem to have forgotten how you rescued me when I was messing things up in the riding arena that day."

She quirked her head, watching him for a long moment. "What are you saying?"

"I am saying…" He paused to choose his words carefully. "I miss you. And you're better at this cowgirl stuff than you think."

"You are stubborn, aren't you?" she said with slight disgust. "You just can't give up on this whole cowgirl-wife thing, can you?"

"Was there a proposal in there somewhere? I thought it was complimenting you. Telling you that I love you, and that you're more important to me than the ranch."

They had stopped dancing again, and were facing each other on the floor, other dancers flowing around them, their eyes wide and curious.

"And," he said slowly, "I'm really glad you didn't wear that damn red lipstick."

He took a step, closing the distance between them as he pulled her into a deep kiss. She froze for a split second before melting into him, her palms against his chest. He felt his shirt tighten when she bunched it in her hands as their kiss continued.

He knew Laura. And he knew that not only did she miss him, but felt as deeply about him as he did about her.

LEVI'S KISS was full of promises and Laura slowly released her grip on his shirt, sliding her right arm around his shoulder as she pressed her left hand to his cheek. The song ended and another started as they continued to kiss.

She had come to Texas with the plan of staying at Luanne's, then the local bed-and-breakfast as she spent more time exploring where to go with her life. But mostly, to figure out whether she and Levi could sort out a way to be together. The cost of the B&B would add up, but it would still be cheaper than providing first and last month's rent for a New York apartment.

"Levi?"

"Hmm?"

"If I'm not a cowgirl helping you out on the ranch, will we ever see each other?" That place was his life—even if he could take a day off to fly to New York.

Levi gave her another kiss, this time bumping their hat brims together in the process. "You are more important than any ranch."

"But it's your livelihood." His identity.

"I gave my brothers an ultimatum about either pitching in or selling their share, so I can get the help I need. I plan to make some changes so I can start having a life again. If you want to hang out around the ranch with me, you can. You're always welcome there. But I also know you have business that takes you to New York and maybe beyond. If you're open to the idea, maybe we could do some short-distance—here in Sweetheart Creek—as well as some long-distance together."

"You don't do long-distance."

"With you I would. Sure, we'll likely get stuck being apart sometimes, but with some flexibility I'm pretty sure we'll find a way to see each other, often enough to keep things working between us."

"There will be times where I'll be away for weeks."

"And there might be nights when I'm out sleeping under the stars, herding cattle."

"And I won't be invited along?"

"I'm not going to assume you'll adopt the cowgirl lifestyle just because we're dating."

"We are?"

"Yes. And if you don't want anything to do with the ranch, that's fine. But if it brings you joy, you go ahead and fit yourself in wherever you like. I trust you."

"Even if I'm wearing the wrong kind of boots?"

He shook his head with an affectionate smile, and she

laughed, then bracketed his face with her hands, kissing him long and slow.

"Thank you," she murmured.

"For what?"

"For accepting the fact that I don't know if I'm coming or going right now."

"You're worth it."

"And that I'm not that perfect cowgirl-wife you're looking for."

"Maybe I've added and subtracted some things on her requirements list."

Laura smiled and adjusted Levi's hat, which had been knocked off-kilter during their kisses.

"So possession happens at Luanne's soon?" he said.

"Yeah."

"Then what?"

"You want a plan, Mr. Levi James Wylder?"

"If you have one."

"I was going to stay at the B&B."

"The B&B?" Brant asked, walking by with a plate of food. "Why?"

She smiled at Levi. "I think I'm going to be in need of a place to stay for a little while."

"You're back?" Henry asked, butting in and scowling at the couple.

"Look, Henry, if you don't—" Levi began.

But his great-uncle interrupted, amazing Levi by saying, "I told Wilma to get her knickers out of those knots and accept this young lady's scholarship. Her boy Donnie needs it."

"What about the stampede, and the need for safety?" Laura asked.

"Betty's coming back in two weeks, I hear. That husband of Janet's should be the actor as far as Betty's concerned. She said he's really milking his injuries, so she's coming home soon so as not to smother him with a pillow. Anyway, I doubt you'll kill anyone before then." He looked grumpy for a long second before adding, "And Levi's a lot happier when you're around. So there's that." He gave his hat a jerk and stalked off.

Laura gazed at Levi in surprise.

"Did you just win him over?" Levi asked. "I don't think anyone's ever done that before."

"There's got to be a catch," Brant said.

Laura shrugged, a wash of relief easing the tension she'd been carrying upon returning to town, fearing what might be said about her or to her. So far people had been welcoming and generally amazing. Not even one joke about the stampede. At least not yet. She figured eventually someone would give in to the temptation.

"Luanne's house is going to be empty for a few weeks after possession," Brant interjected. He caught Levi's stormy look and said quickly, "Life happens, man."

"Who did you buy that house for?" Levi demanded. He'd been thinking it was for April, but he wasn't so sure that added up. Was there a secret woman somewhere? A niece or nephew he didn't know about? The very idea riled him.

Brant ignored him, addressing Laura. "If you want, you can stay for a few weeks more, maybe a month or two. It might be easier and cheaper than changing the possession date."

"What would the rent be?"

"Less than anything in New York, for sure. We can figure something out. In the meantime, enjoy the dance." Skillfully balancing his plate of food, he lifted his hat and gave a half bow before slipping into the crowd.

"Well, that solves that problem," Levi said, watching his brother walk away.

"I'll cancel my reservation at the local bed-and-breakfast," Laura said with a smile.

"You're staying!" Jackie cried, throwing her arms around

Laura. Apparently her friend had been eavesdropping. She caught Levi's look and backed away, hands raised. "Sorry. I just really had to know firsthand how things were going to end for you two."

Levi shook his head in exasperation and Laura giggled.

"So you made a reservation?" Levi asked.

"I had a feeling I might find a reason to stay a little longer than I have the house for."

"Well, I plan to give you a reason to stay a good while longer than you can rent that place, too," Levi said, pulling her in for another delicious kiss.

SEVERAL WEEKS LATER, Laura leaned against the fence out behind the ranch house with Levi, sipping coffee from an enamel coffee cup that matched his. There was something magical about watching the dew evaporate at dawn, a cup of coffee in your hand and the man you loved standing beside you.

Betty had returned yesterday, happily bustling about the stables. Laura had been helping out, fitting herself into activities here and there. Tomorrow she had to head to New York for a photo shoot for the perfume packaging, as well as a few meetings.

Laura and Levi had been taking things as they came, catching themselves when they started making assumptions.

"You gonna marry me?" Levi asked now, turning to face her.

"Are you going to come to New York to watch the photo shoot?" she countered. He would be a fish out of water, and she'd love to see how he handled the hustle of the city as well as her job.

"Is your yes contingent on mine?"

"No. But if we're throwing wild and crazy ideas out there..."

"You want me underfoot?" He raised his eyebrows doubtfully.

She'd figured he would stay here, but the more she thought about it, the more she wanted him to come along.

"I don't think you could handle being underfoot," she said, pretending to be deep in thought.

"If you want me there, I will be."

"Who will take care of the ranch?"

"Brant opened his big mouth the other day. He said I create most of the problems around here. I think it would do him good if I went away and left him in charge."

"What would he do with his veterinary office?"

"I don't know."

"Most of the ranch work would fall on Myles, wouldn't it?"

"It might."

"Does that freak you out?"

"The fact that I wouldn't be in charge, and that things might not get done the way I'd like them to?" He inhaled sharply, setting his coffee cup on a fence post. "It freaks me out like you would not believe."

"It would probably be good for you."

"It might. The new hired hand seems to be working out well, and Hank's not too worried about me leaving, so…" He shrugged.

Target zipped past on his long, retractable leash, chasing an orange kitten, which stopped suddenly, back arched as it hissed and swiped at the dog. The mother cat came barreling out of nowhere, sending Target racing back to Laura. She set down her cup and caught him when he jumped up, and Levi reached over to scratch him behind the ears. She'd been taking him to classes for ranch dogs and he was getting better, but still had a lot to learn.

"My dad used to get away from the ranch sometimes when we were kids," Levi said. "We would go to Indigo Bay and play in the ocean for a few weeks each summer."

"That's where my photo shoot was!"

Levi smiled. "My uncle Danny would take over the ranch

while we were gone. I remember coming back. There would always be so much to do, but that time away was really special."

"Why did you stop going?"

"Danny was struck and killed by a drunk driver."

"I'm so sorry to hear that."

"Yeah." Levi gazed into the distance for a moment, remembering how at the funeral the five brothers had taken a barely spoken vow to never drive after even one drink. As far as he knew, they were all keeping to it.

Laura gave his arm a squeeze, and he smiled at her. "When's our flight?"

She squealed, hugging Target close. "Really?"

"Yeah. Why not?" He grinned, sliding an arm around her, placing a kiss on her forehead. "I think it would do me some good to see how you've been living all these years. No fresh air. No hot cowboys. What a hardship you must have faced. It's probably a good thing I came along to save you from that sad fate."

"Prepare to have your mind blown, Princess."

"Who are you calling a princess?"

She laughed and tried to slip away, but he pulled her into a long, lingering kiss that made her believe in happily ever afters.

MYLES WYLDER WONDERED what on earth he was doing. He closed the football coaching textbook and pushed away from the kitchen table in the ranch house. Levi had gone to New York with Laura a few days ago, leaving Brant, Ryan and him in charge of the place.

So far Brant and Myles had been run off their feet. Meanwhile, Ryan was Ryan. He'd hired a teen from their football team to do his hour or two of morning chores, and was enjoying his time off. As usual.

The real question was how Levi got so much done in a day.

Even with the new hired hand in place tasks were stacking up on the brothers. Now he understood why Levi was so eager to get the ranch's future sorted out. That and to get Cole to return home. In any case, if Levi kept taking off with Laura like this, they were going to need a plan. Especially since the ranch work was cutting into Myles's much-needed study time.

Nobody knew he was upgrading his coaching credentials, which meant he wasn't getting any support. But it also meant nobody would taunt him when he inevitably flunked.

Myles tugged Levi's long list of things to do from under the fridge magnet. As he looked at the words, the letters ran together, no longer making sense. He rubbed his eyes, knowing he was tired, then crumpled the list in his fist. He had most of it memorized from when Levi had gone over it, anyway.

Myles stuffed his textbook into his backpack, shaking his head. He'd made it through high school, then vowed to never return. And here he was. Taking a class. But better credentials meant higher pay, and a greater ability to help out the ranch by pulling a smaller salary from it, and that was good. Plus he wanted to prove to Karen Hartley, the school and town librarian, that he wasn't just a jockhead.

If he was going to pass—and he was—he needed a plan of attack. No tutors, unlike in high school. But because it was an online course, it also meant no teachers verbally going over the lessons. Just a textbook, online readings, and lots of typed up discussion.

Maybe the distraction of a drink at the Watering Hole would help him figure things out.

As Myles drove up Main Street in Sweetheart Creek, he prepared to park in front of the saloon, but then changed his mind and continued on past, hanging a left at the gas station as though heading to the high school football field. He slowed while passing the library, where Karen worked. It was late. He was just providing a security check, that was all. Nothing creepy.

Karen's compact car was the only one in the small paved lot. As he watched, the library door opened and Karen backed out, lugging a large box in her arms. Myles swung into the lot, turned off his truck and hopped out. With long strides he caught up with her and took the carton.

"Myles!" Her cheeks grew pink and her eyes glittered with pleasure behind her black-framed glasses. "You're like a superhero cowboy, appearing whenever I need help."

"Yup."

She popped her trunk and he put the heavy box inside. "Your weekend's books-to-be-read pile just got bigger?"

She gave that light laugh of hers that always made his heart feel warmer. "I love that you know what a TBR pile is. And no, I'm processing these discards to sell online, to help raise money for the library."

"In your spare time?" Shouldn't she be paid for that?

"If I don't do this in my spare time, it'll create more of it—if you know what I mean?"

"I don't."

"There have been more funding restrictions and cutbacks. The town is talking about completely shutting down the library, so I'm trying to help bring in a little money by selling these library books that are no longer needed or wanted in the collection."

"I thought they were just shortening the library's operating hours." That's what his mom had said when her book club night had changed from Thursdays to Fridays.

The sadness in Karen's eyes told him that major cuts were on the horizon.

"That's wrong," he said.

"You say that like you plan to correct it." She gave a nervous laugh, toying with the top button of her blouse.

"I do."

She seemed amused by his indignation. "And what would this

big burly cowboy do to save the library?" She seemed slightly breathless as she said that, and Myles felt his heart give an irregular thump in response.

"We'd do something. Together."

"You make it sound simple."

"Maybe it is."

She dropped her hand to her side. "I don't think so."

"You think we can't?"

She studied him, her eyes serious behind those sexy glasses. He wondered what she looked like without them. Would she be as cute, or look as though her appearance was missing something?

"I...hadn't really thought about it."

"How much funding does the library need?"

She said the number like it was a sin. The total required to keep the doors open, the shelves stocked, as well as cover her salary was a paltry sum compared to what he'd imagined.

"What? Don't they pay you?" he teased. "That's barely more than they pay us football coaches."

She gave a wry smile that brought her lips into a tight rosebud —one he longed to kiss, to see if it would open into that large, easy smile he so dearly loved.

"The town council is good at making it clear where their values are."

"The library does a lot for this community," Myles countered.

"So does football."

He couldn't tell if she was being cynical or not, but guessed that she was. "It's not the same."

"You're right."

He looked at the fieldstone building with its arched entryway and large old-fashioned windows. It had likely once oozed charm, but was now looking sad and neglected, the grounds overrun with weeds and half-dead shrubs—unlike the school's football field, which had recently received some upgrades thanks to the town. "Double that number."

"Double it?" Karen scoffed, obviously feeling that amount could never be raised.

"Yeah. Double." In his mind's eye he could see the small, but significant fixes that would bring this building back to life. Make it the community hub it deserved to be. The library, he knew, was more than just a nice place to sit and read, or for those who wanted a computer class in the evening, or for moms and their little ones who needed an outing. He'd heard his mother talk about it, and he knew that if Karen believed in this place, then saving it was worth every ounce of effort it would take.

"You're going to need to freshen this place up. And maybe add a self-serve coffee bar."

"We have a self-serve coffee bar."

"Oh." It had been a while since he'd been in the library, as the former head librarian had been a bit of a lizard. She'd been wrinkly and long faced in a way that always made him feel unwelcome, and as though he didn't belong there. Which was true. "You also need a raise."

Karen laughed.

"What? Did that number include your annual salary?"

She looked away as though ashamed.

He crossed his arms. "You need to earn more than you do. Speak up for yourself. Don't accept this crap."

"Myles!" She looked surprised by his tone.

"If you don't teach them how you expect to be treated they'll never pay you what you're worth."

"And what am I worth?" She had her own arms crossed, hip out, challenging him in a way that made him want to pull out the pencil she'd twirled into her hair, toss it across the parking lot and kiss her senseless. He angled his body closer, inhaling her scent. She straightened her spine as though prepared to fight.

He locked his gaze on her lips for a second, then lifted his eyes to hers. "You're worth everything."

She blushed from the neckline of her blouse right up to her hairline. Her mouth opened before she swallowed the smile that had started. This woman didn't get complimented nearly often enough.

"So?" he asked quietly, the evening air quiet around them. "What do you say? Will you consider my proposal?"

"To save the library?" she asked, her voice uneven.

"Yes. You and me."

"You and me," she echoed weakly. Her fingers had gone back to worrying her buttons.

He shifted like he was going to move in for a kiss and she inhaled swiftly, her chin tipping up too fast. There was too much uncertainty, too much thinking going on in that brain of hers. She was interested and intrigued, but he wanted more than that. He wanted her to be sure, sure enough to free herself, let go and be in the moment with him. Not just engage in one kiss and then act as though it had never happened.

"I...I don't think you and I would work. On the library. Together. As a team. To save it." She smoothed her blouse, backing away, eyes darting anywhere but at him.

"Karen? We can."

Her eyes met his immediately, so hopeful and yet so uncertain. He needed to find a way to make her notice him as more than the football-loving cowboy who appeared at the right time to lift heavy things.

He needed to convince her to let him help. If he could get her to say yes to working on saving the library together, then maybe she would begin to see him in a new light. As a man she wanted to be with.

His plan could work as long as she didn't discover the one thing that might cause her to say no. The one thing this beautiful and bright librarian didn't suspect.

THE COWBOY'S OF SWEETHEART CREEK, TEXAS

Read them all!

The Cowboy's Stolen Heart (Levi)

The Cowboy's Secret Wish (Myles)

The Cowboy's Second Chance (Ryan)

The Cowboy's Sweet Elopement (Brant)

The Cowboy's Surprise Return (Cole)

There are more Sweetheart Creek stories set in Indigo Bay! Maria has her own special story, Sweet Joymaker. Their cousin Nick's story is Sweet Troublemaker. And you can't forget about the Wylders' cousin Alexa! Her story is Sweet Holiday Surprise.

Indigo Bay

Sweet romances set in a beach town—meet characters new and old in this spinoff series.

Sweet Matchmaker (Ginger and Logan)

Sweet Holiday Surprise (Cash & Alexa)

Sweet Forgiveness (Ashton & Zoe)

Sweet Troublemaker (Nick & Polly)

Sweet Joymaker (Maria & Clint)

ABOUT THE AUTHOR

Jean Oram is a *New York Times* and *USA Today* bestselling romance author. Inspiration for her small town series came from her own upbringing on the Canadian prairies. Although, so far, none of her characters have grown up in an old schoolhouse or worked on a bee farm. Jean still lives on the prairie with her husband, two kids, and big shaggy dog where she can be found out playing in the snow or hiking.

Become an Official Fan:
www.facebook.com/groups/jeanoramfans
Newsletter: www.jeanoram.com/FREEBOOK
Twitter: www.twitter.com/jeanoram
Instagram: www.instagram.com/author_jeanoram
Facebook: www.facebook.com/JeanOramAuthor
Website & blog: www.jeanoram.com